Praise for T. V. Olsen's
The Stalking Moon

"A masterful job of winding historical moments of the West into a real, suspenseful drama."
—*Lewiston, Maine, Journal*

"Exciting . . . handled with skill and feeling."
—*Pittsburgh Press*

"Sam—He Was Here"

"I know. What did he do?"

Sara sat upright, clutching his arms. "Now he knows," she whispered. "God help us!"

Vetch shook her. "What did he do?"

"He—nothing. Just this." She touched the bruise. A hint of something cowed and hopeless lay in her face, and he did not like to see it.

She murmured, "He said that when he sees me again, he will cut off my nose. He is not ready yet." Vetch only nodded; that was the traditional retribution allowed the cuckolded Apache husband. "And he said to tell you somthing, Sam. That he is in no hurry. He said—he said that you started to die when you killed Susto, but you did not know it. You will go on dying for a time yet because he wants you to know it."

The Stalking Moon

T. V. OLSEN

LEISURE BOOKS NEW YORK CITY

A LEISURE BOOK®

May 2010

Published by special arrangement with Golden West Literary Agency.

Dorchester Publishing Co., Inc.
200 Madison Avenue
New York, NY 10016

ISBN 10: 0-8439-4180-4
ISBN 13: 978-0-8439-4180-7

The name "Leisure Books" and the stylized "L" with design are trademarks of Dorchester Publishing Co., Inc.

Printed in the United States of America.

10 9 8 7 6 5 4 3 2 1

Visit us online at www.dorchesterpub.com.

The
Stalking
Moon

Chapter One

The detachment was a half day out of Fort Sutro, bearing southeast, when it angled onto the
northbound trail of Toriano's band. Nick Tana,
the half-Apache scout, cut the renegades' sign
on the muddy bank of San Simon Creek when
the column halted to water; he pointed it out to
Sam Vetch, chief scout.

Vetch stood a few yards off, letting his rawboned pinto dip its muzzle into the slimy strag-
gle of water that ran a scant inch deep where it
did not stand in stagnant pools. He turned his
head briefly, saying, "Lieutenant," in his soft
Southern voice that somehow carried easily
over the heterogeneous sounds of muttered
voices, clinking metal, and creaking leather that
marked a troop halt.

Unhurriedly then, Vetch finished watering

the pinto. He was a long, lean man, gaunt in the way a puma is, standing easily hipshot with a rare kind of angular grace. His clothes, faded duck trousers, a calico shirt discolored by alkali and sweat salt, and stiff-toed hip-length moccasins folded down at the knee, were softened by wear and age and fitted his bone-hard frame with a shabby comfort. His taciturn Nordic face was oddly like an Indian's, bony and high-cheekboned, sun-blackened nearly to the color and texture of old saddle leather worn smooth, except for the deep sun wrinkles at the corners of his eyes. They were strange eyes to meet first, an off-shade gray-green and squinted from scanning distances. When he took off his hat to sleeve his forehead his chestnut hair lay tight and sweat-curly against his skull where it did not shag over his neck and ears in ragged fantails; deep streaks of grizzled gray added a piebald effect. Sam Vetch had the never-young look of a man used and seasoned in harsh and endless rigors, but also the not-old look of an out-doorsman; he might have passed for ten years to either side of his true age, which was thirty-seven.

He let the pinto drink only briefly; he never pampered the animal, which was desert-bred and could live when necessity demanded on cholla or on prickly pear with the spines burned away. He picketed the horse and straightened about as Lieutenant McPartland left off talking with Sergeant Rudabaugh and, holding his saber high, clambered down over the splintered

red boulders rimming the creek bank.

Vetch motioned toward Nick Tana, who was lazily waving the troopers and their horses away from the patch of trampled mud where the tracks were. He glanced at Vetch and McPartland as they came up.

"Toriano?" McPartland asked.

"Himself, he passed here a good day ago," Nick Tana said. "Him and his men. Not the women, though. Their tracks ain't over three hours old—women and small kids. A few old men."

Vetch had dropped to his hunkers to scan the sign, and now he lifted his head. "And babies. You figure he's in a hurry, Nick?"

Nick Tana nodded. "He ain't gathering no moss. There was a whisper around San Carlos that Nachita and Loco might bust out. Reckon by now they have."

Lieutenant McPartland had also squatted down by the tracks, and he looked up, mystified. "Babies?"

Vetch pointed at some indentations in the mud at the base of the rock. "A woman leaned her *tsoch* there. Rig for toting a baby on her back, made of mesquite branches and rawhide. You can see the thong marks."

"I don't see a damned thing," the lieutenant said. "Now, about these San Carlos chiefs that may break reservation—you mean that Toriano will join them?"

His rueful grin altered to a searching gravity that made his smooth face older than its twenty-three years warranted. He was, Vetch knew, the youngest junior officer at Fort Sutro; newly assigned to the frontier and generally full of the devil, he was taking his first command with a deadly sobriety.

"Keep an eye on him, Sam," was all that Major Kinship had said back at Sutro; but it was no accident that the commandant had sent his chief scout with McPartland's detail. The major knew from reports of Toriano's depredations below the border only that the Chiricahua chief had come out of the Sierra Madre where he had withdrawn over a decade ago. From here his warriors had made short raids into the Mexican settlements, looting their terrorized populations with contemptuous ease. The rich, goods-laden *conductas* out of Hermosillo that supplied the wealthy *haciendados* had also offered easy prey. Only recently had the Mexican army moved in force against Toriano, causing him to push north. The nearly unbroken line of his lightning raids indicated his intention of crossing into the States at a point in the Sierra Rica foothills. That might be exactly what the canny Toriano wanted the Americans to think; his true cross point might be many miles to the east or west.

The army wanted Toriano intercepted, if possible, before his bloody hand fell on the border and southern settlements and ranches. The commandant of Fort Sutro, the southernmost outpost, had had no choice but to splinter his undermanned command in order to fan out troops in three directions. Captain Bellew, an old-guard Indian fighter, took his troops due south toward Toriano's ostensible crossing at the Rica foothills. Lieutenant Courteen, also a veteran in Apache country, was sent to cover the southwest approach. And, with his two remaining officers out of action, one furloughed, and the other down sick, Major Kinship had no choice but to send downy-cheeked Second Lieutenant McPartland toward the southeast. The young Pointer had some patrols and a brush or two with hostiles to his credit; it was not lack of confidence in McPartland, who had so far acquitted himself well, but rather ignorance of his untried capacity for leadership that had prompted the major to send along Sam Vetch.

"That would be why he's in a hurry," Vetch said to McPartland's query. "If his young men are impatient Toriano couldn't hold them back. That would be the only reason they'd let the women fall behind. If Nachita and Loco made their break today, and you can depend on Nick's having the straight of that, Toriano and his warriors must be in a rush to rendezvous with them—say, early tomorrow."

Nick Tana nodded agreement, coming in a lithe movement to his feet, a slim and indolent young man a few years the lieutenant's elder. His mixed blood showed in the light skin that was the legacy of a Yankee trader whose name he had never known and the Athapascan features bequeathed him by his Apache mother, who, Nick claimed, was the daughter of the great war chief Tana. Nick wore a blue army blouse and a battered black campaign hat, but from the waist down he was an Apache warrior, in breechclout and hip-length moccasins of white deerskin with the stiff, upcurling toe. His background too was hybrid; mission-educated, he worked for the army but spent most of his time with his mother's relatives on reservation. As a go-between, Major Kinship considered Nick Tana invaluable. As a tracker he could run rings around either of the fullbood Apache scouts who had accompanied Bellew's and Courteen's details. And as a friend Sam Vetch considered him second to none.

"How the devil," McPartland muttered, scrubbing a bandanna across his sweating neck, "do they get word back and forth?"

"Runner," Nick said. " 'Pache can jog up forty miles after running his horse to death, Lieutenant, no time out but to eat some of the horse. There's lone hostiles slipping on and off San Carlos all the time,'most always to see relations. It ain't much trouble."

"God," Lieutenant McPartland said quietly, beginning to assess the implications of the problem. "Rudabaugh! Map on the double over here."

Sergeant Rudabaugh was watering his own mount and McPartland's, and he bawled for a trooper to hold the reins. He took a leather case from the lieutenant's saddlebag and came over, his wiry big-shouldered body swinging in an

14

easy half lope but in no particular hurry. Rudabaugh's wry, puckered face, pouched by an omnipresent wad of tobacco, held an unutterable patience; his favorite complaint was that he could never serve a hitch and quit because C Troop always had a new shavetail to be broken in.

McPartland opened the case and took out a folded field map, which crackled as he unfolded it. He sank back on his haunches and spread the map on his knees, and Vetch and Nick Tana squatted on either side of him. Rudabaugh stood behind them, slablike hands cocked on his hips as he peered between their shoulders.

The vast sprawl of San Carlos, the northern reservation that held over four thousand contented or restive Apaches, was outlined in red ink. Just below its southern boundary lay Fort Thomas; to the southwest was Fort Bowie; and Fort Sutro was situated deep to the southeast. The three forts formed a fairly regular triangle whose area embraced hundreds of square miles of desert and mountain.

McPartland traced a finger northward along the wavering line of San Simon Creek. "He's following it roughly, would you say?"

Vetch grunted and tapped a blunt finger on the creek line at the approximate center of the fort-cornered triangle. "Would put 'em around here by now. They have about a twenty-five hour lead on you."

"Damn," McPartland murmured. "If we had started out just a day earlier we could have intercepted him directly. If he joins forces with Nachita and Loco and their combined bands are turned loose on the territory—Damn, we could never catch them before they rendez-vous."

"Begging the Lieutenant's pardon." Ruda-baugh's voice came soft and utterly bland. "Thomas will have a force on the trail of them Injuns that busted reservation, more'n enough to hit them hard if need be."

"Very likely, Sergeant," McPartland said with some asperity. "My orders are still to intercept Toriano and engage him if necessary—"

"True, sir, but having slipped past us by many hours he is now deep in the mountains. No longer a question of interception, sir, but of pursuit. Now I'm afraid—"

"That'll do, Sergeant."

"Yes, sir, Mister McPartland," Rudabaugh barked softly.

The young officer lifted a bright and angry glance to the sergeant's totally closed expression, but any reprimand died unvoiced. The noncom would use the qualifying "mister," the easy address of high rank to a second lieutenant, only to register unusually strong disapproval. The inference was too plain, and McPartland flushed and lowered his eyes to the map.

He could not quite voice the apology that must now preface a deference to his sergeant's opinion, but he back-tracked indirectly by saying, "What do you think, Mr. Vetch? My orders did not rule out pursuit; it was left to my discretion."

"Why," Vetch said mildly, "I'd make it good sense if Toriano and his boys had, say, only a three-four hour lead and you wanted to gamble on running them down in short order."

He said no more, throwing it squarely back in McPartland's lap. The lieutenant groaned under his breath; he kneaded his knuckles gently along his teeth, staring at the map. Vetch sympathized with his dilemma; an encounter with Toriano meant a golden chance to acquit himself highly on his first field command. But running down Toriano before his manpower was tripled by joining with the reservation breakaways was out of the question, and to overtake him at all McPartland would have to set a horse-killing day-and-night pace that would leave his men dead spent, in no shape for battle.

Then McPartland gave Vetch a sharp, abrupt glance. "If they had a three-or four-hour lead, you say. And Tana said that the women and children are just three hours away . . . Is *that* your idea?"

"They're moving slow, and afoot too. My idea, round up the women and kids and take 'em to San Carlos. Meantime the big garrison from Fort Thomas will be running the warriors to ground. The young bucks are in a fighting mood and they'll outrun the army, like always, till they feel like coming in quietly. When Toriano's boys hear their families have already been moved to reservation, it could just discourage 'em a heap sooner. And the women and kids being of Toriano's band, you'd be acting inside orders, Lieutenant."

"Why yes." McPartland's lips twisted wryly. "Intercepting them."

There was hardly glory in loose herding a crowd of hostile, sullen females and children, and to a young lieutenant spoiling for a fight the choice was a bitter one, Vetch knew. Sergeant Rudabaugh's face was a wry study as he waited the officer's reply, and then McPartland sighed. "All right—all right. The prudent thing, of course." Vetch saw Rudabaugh's face relax slightly before he turned away, his judgment vindicated.

In saddle again the detachment moved due north at an acute angle now to their former route, once more traversing the alkaline flats of a vast *playa* they had crossed only that morning. The sky was a hot blue magnet drawing the moisture from a man's tissues, the sullen press of heat laying like a dead hand on his body and spirits. Dust devils danced far away and close by, gusting in ragged plumes of bone-dry dust that grittily powdered every square inch of a man's hide, sifting over and inside his clothing. Even his eyeballs grated when he moved them, and his vision danced with white dazzling pinpoints of heat.

Riding ahead of the sweltering column, the need for vigilance relaxed on the naked flat, Sam Vetch let the idle drift of his thoughts fix with longing on the Soledad River country of

New Mexico and his ranch there. He smelled the dark spicy green of cool firs and pines mantling the mountain flanks; he saw the creaming torrent of a rock-laced stream rushing past his tight log house, built between the granite cliffs where it would be warm in winter, cool in summer; he tasted the earthy ice-coldness of water from the spring that bubbled below it.

It was hard to believe that his long-dreamed-of home in that distant high country was at last a fact. He had always liked wintering in those mountains, tramping and hunting and fishing in spring and fall, and long ago he had sized up his ideal of a homesite. Vetch had poured the savings of many years and dozens of grueling desert scoutings into buying his land and building on it to last, stocking his rich-grassed slopes with a small herd of Herefords. That, and intermittent spells of backbreaking work and sweat.

Now the place was ready for its future tenants, and Sam Vetch did not have to ask himself whether he was ready for it; he knew. He had been a scout for the army in one capacity or another since his twenty-second year, and fifteen years of it was enough for any man. Harsh and lonely as the life could be, it held a romantic appeal to youth and to any man who could draw deep, serene resources from wilderness living. His new life, ranching twenty miles from the nearest neighbor, would likewise reflect that part of Vetch's nature, but a man needed more. . . .

More was the woman a man built for, the center of his home and whatever meaning he assigned to his life. Without this, the rest would be an empty thing; and so Vetch's reflections took a worried turn. *I should have asked her before, I reckon. She is a gentle lady, Miss Vangie is, and it will be all different for her, a mite rough. I have taken on a lot of rough edges I will have to wear down. She favors me plain enough, rough edges and all. But a man should make sure of a woman, all the same. First thing I get back to Silverton, I will.* They could be married by the circuit preacher and be on their way to his ranch within a few days if Miss Evangeline Armitage were willing. He fervently hoped that his suddenly pressing the question after this long delay would not make her feel that she was being taken lightly or for granted.

Strange to think that this was the last scout, that in a few days he would be free to pick up his final army check and leave a way of life that had become unthinking habit. It gave a man somewhat of the fluttering fantods he felt on topping an unfamiliar hill in unknown country. Yet, wondering if he could come to terms with a drastic change in his way of life, he thought with a fair certainty that whatever residue of wild oats remained in his system could be easily checkreined. Youth was restlessness and quick temper and a selfish indifference to all outside itself. The years brought home to a man the need to husband his energies for something worthwhile and not be a cheap gambler with his life and abilities. At such a point he ceased quietly to ridicule other men's dependence on home and wife, seeing the goodness these things wrought in them and finding wellsprings of gentleness and tolerance released in him by the realization. And his own need followed from that.

The trouble with finding something to live for was that you could become too damned prudent. Vetch had known his moments of queasy excitement; he had never conceded any sense of fear as such, though he had seen men afraid, breaking and running or going stiff in buck fever. Like any man of good upbringing and some education thrown back on his own thoughts by gradual aging in a lonely life, Vetch had occasionally, curiously, wondered how fear might come to him and how he would know it and how he might react. Now he was getting an inkling.

By learning what life could mean he had sloughed off an old fatalism and become vulnerable. Where his imagination and lore had once provoked cautious assessments of a given situation, he now found himself starting at odd moments and finding odd symptoms in his hairtrigger pulse and dry throat. Since fear was normal in most men going to war, he supposed that these were normal signs, having as source a blind concern that this last time he would face old, routine dangers would also be the time that a stray or directed slug or arrow would bear his name. A phlegmatic man, he had seen enough of life's savage ironies to be sure of no talisman;

but neither was he superstitious and that he could not shrug away the nagging thought annoyed him.

Well out ahead of the column, Nick Tana easily followed the well-defined trail, half bent sideways from horseback. Only when the *playa* began to break up into thrusting, eroded mesas crosshatched by shallow canyons did the half-breed frequently dismount to check the ground. As the ridges grew rougher and the canyons deeper and more tortuous, Vetch fell back by McPartland.

He said, "Lieutenant, next rest halt, when you change flankers and detail positions, you had best throw them flankers out farther. Ambush terrain."

"All right." McPartland prodded his hat off his forehead and sleeved gray dust from his face. His eyes were puffy from the heat. "I've held in because you said the women and young ones would travel slow. Just when do we overtake them? It'll be dark before long."

"All the better. They won't move after dark. Bad medicine. You can likely catch 'em asleep then. All of a 'Pache's training, Lieutenant, is toward never letting an enemy surprise him. Catch him off his guard and he don't know how to take it; then you got him where the hair is short."

"I'm not sure we should try to overtake them now. Our horses are nearly played out."

Vetch thought a moment. "There's a seep up ahead, at the mouth of Crenna Canyon. It ain't good water, but a critter or a 'Pache can keep it down. A near sure bet they'll camp there. Would say you'd be safe in halting now and laying up a couple hours. When it cools off you can travel fast and catch up soon."

McPartland hesitated only a moment before complying, calling the halt in a dry wash that held enough mesquite brush for firewood. The guards were posted, and the men built fires to cook their bacon; they munched hardtack and washed it down with water from their canteens. When twilight fading to dusk brought relief from the heat, McPartland ordered them to saddle again.

Vetch took his bearings by landmarks and checked them with Nick Tana, and the two led the column northeast through the growing darkness. For nearly an hour the murmurous grousing and sullen curses of the exhausted troopers and the noises of horses moving on rock formed the only breaks in the night stillness.

The horses, scenting water, gave the first restless indications that the seep was near. Vetch judged that it lay beyond the next ridge. After telling McPartland to rest the column, he dismounted and handed Nick his reins and went ahead on foot. The crumbling talus of the ridge side was treacherous; against any giveaway sound he made a slow and cautious ascent and dropped to his belly at the summit.

The valley was no more than an oval dimple in the vast upheaval of this range. At its far end the mouth of Crenna Canyon was a maw of black shadow. The seep welled from the base of the ridge on this side, the light of a banked fire plying the black water with wan glimmers. He counted at least thirty blanketed forms around the fire, and as he watched, one of them stirred and rose to add more greasewood to the fire.

Vetch's eyes narrowed. This was not a woman or an old one, but a squat, muscular bull of a man in his prime. Probably Toriano had left behind several picked warriors to guard the women. Vetch had seen plenty of horse sign, and of course the warriors had all been mounted.

He inched backward on his belly off skyline, then descended to where the detail waited. "There's grass in the canyon," he told McPartland. "That's where their horses are. Better cut them off before you order a charge."

McPartland told the men to remove their spurs, and he and Vetch led off upslope. Just below the ridge crest the lieutenant sent Sergeant Rudabaugh and five troopers to the right to skirt between the sleeping camp and the horses. He deployed the remaining troopers in a skirmish line and they went up and over the summit in almost total silence.

At the first stir of alarmed movement, below, McPartland ordered a charge. A buck lunged for the fire to scatter it; Nick Tana hauled up and, butting his rifle to his shoulder, dropped the man in his tracks.

The troopers boiled off the last off taper of

slope, and shots peppered the fire-splashed night as the line rolled over the camp. There was more wild confusion than shooting, for McPartland had warned them not to shoot at women or children, to try to capture the handful of bucks alive, to make sure of their targets before returning fire.

A group of women, brought out of their blankets by the pandemonium, huddled to one side. Vetch's glance was pulled that way as one woman broke away from the others with a low cry. She was running forward, clutching something to her breast, when another woman started after her—and was almost on her when Vetch saw firelight flash wickedly off a knife blade. It was poised in the raised fist of the second woman, and before she could plunge it into the other's back, Vetch brought his pistol level and shot.

The second dropped to her knees with a bitter, howling cry; the first woman halted, turning in her confusion, and as she half faced the fire Vetch realized that the bundle she carried was a baby. He had only time to register a fleeting impression of stumbling onto something damned strange when the mellow voice of Sergeant Rudabaugh boomed its warning, "Watch yourself, laddy buck!"

Vetch came pivoting around on his heel, catching movement from the corners of his eyes. He saw a man, the squat and muscular man he had noted earlier, lunging in low and silent from the side, a quartz-shod lance lined even with Vetch's belly. The scout palmed his gun around and his shot merged with the bellow of Rudabaugh's big service revolver. The buck spun under the impact of the bullets, and as he went down his thick arm backed by his massive weight thrust the lance in a spasmodic fury that furrowed the weapon's head deep into the ground ahead of Vetch's foot.

Vetch stepped backward, instinctively dropping his gun muzzle. Then, seeing that the man was dead, he swung his attention around the camp. The situation was already in hand except on the far slope, where two or three bucks were in retreat, firing at the pursuing troopers.

Vetch let a breath of vague jubilation sigh out of his lungs. The skirmish was finished, the last skirmish for him, and he could grin at his misgivings; he was alive and free for the new life. Just now had been a damned near thing, so near that he could almost believe that he had been deliberately spared.

He looked again at the woman with the baby. She had not moved from where she had stopped, but now a boy of about eight had come up and was standing half in front of her. Her free hand, the one not holding the baby, rested on the boy's shoulder, and it was hard to say who was protecting whom. Firelight flashed against the boy's dark fierce eyes and he was straight as a young pine; there was no fear in him.

Sergeant Rudabaugh stepped up beside Vetch, punching the spent loads from his revolver. He eyed the woman carefully, and more briefly the children, and said phlegmatically, "I'm thinking we rescued ourselves some white people from the devils." And then, peering closer at the baby and the boy, he exclaimed softly, "Ah, now there is a case! But at least she is white."

The woman's eyes were grave and unchanging; she said nothing, but her hand pulled the boy against her skirt and held him tightly.

Chapter Two

Vetch stepped from Fort Sutro's one-room hospital at a corner of the parade grounds, and out of consideration for the freshly sowed grass skirted it by way of the gravel walk. He had spent a pleasant hour chatting with Nick Tana, who had taken a bullet in the thigh while cutting the Apache males off from their retreat. The two days in the saddle that followed had been brutal ones for Nick, who, rather than ride directly back to Fort Sutro and care, had stayed with the detail on its slow return to the fort, escorting Toriano's women and children and old people. Here they would be held until they were moved north to San Carlos.

Heading for the adobe headquarters building that made up one side of the west sentry gate, Vetch glanced down toward the forage sheds where the Apache captives huddled apathetically in the afternoon sunlight. For years he had tracked hostiles because it was the work he did best and his talent commanded good pay. Since it had never been a case of liking the job, he had found it essential to grow a shell of pitiless composure toward the people he had hunted. Lately enough gentleness had touched Vetch's life to buckle the shell, and let him pity these remnants of a proud-fierce people.

The parade ground drowsed under the sun; the young cottonwoods lining the gravel walk rustled in a hot breeze as Vetch turned up a short path to the headquarters building, stirring his shoulders against a twinging cramp. He had slept almost the clock around in the bachelor officers' quarters, but he no longer came back with the green resiliency of youth.

Probably that fact had underscored the other reasons he was quitting the game; he had known one too many nights of stray pebbles gouging his hide through his ground blanket, one too few drinks left in the canteen before the next water, one too many tiring hills climbed for the dreary sameness of just another side. It was well ended, and nothing remained but to pick up his last check, bid farewell to a few old friends, and board the next stage to Silverton—and Miss Vangie Armitage.

Entering, Vetch crossed the anteroom and said to Sergeant Severn behind the desk, "How, Mike. The C.O. in?"

"He is," the sergeant said morosely. "Occupied for the nonce, though. You've come for your pay, I presume?"

Vetch nodded.

"The adjutant's office has already made out your check," Sergeant Severn said, taking it from a desk drawer, "but the major has to sign it."

"That's all right," Vetch said. "I'll come back later." He wheeled and started out, and then halted as the inner office door opened.

"Heard you talking, Sam," Major Kinship said. "Would you step in here? Afraid I need your help one last time."

Vetch nodded and went past the major into the office, curiosity in him. It was a bare room except for a desk and two chairs and, standing in opposite corners, the American flag and the squadron standard. A woman occupied one of the chairs, and it took Vetch a full three seconds to recognize her.

He had last seen her in the shapeless calico dress and leggins of an Apache woman; her dark brown hair, now braided in a glossy coronet around her head, had been done in the Apache fashion. Now she was wearing a faded gingham dress, probably given her by the commandant's wife. It was several sizes too large for her, though she was a tall and big-boned woman. An Apache diet did not lend itself to excess pounds, particularly on an Anglo-Saxon frame.

She would be something less than attractive even in well-fitting clothes; the protruding lines of collarbone above the dress hinted at the emaciation below that. Her hands and face were gaunt, and her skin was tanned almost to an Indian darkness and would have been leathery with a few more years' captivity. Yet even at first glance her height and hair and features had proclaimed her obviously white. Of her Apache dress she had retained only the moccasins, which peeped past the skirt hem; it would be a time before her feet were again comfortable in shoes.

Major Kinship seated himself behind his desk and picked up a pencil, frowning at it. He was a whip-lean man of erect carriage, with black full mustaches flecked by a gray frost that matched his eyes. He was no garrison soldier and just this side of a martinet, but out of sight of his troops he was the most human of men. He looked at the woman, a troubled compassion in his face. "Miss, er, Miss Carver—"

"Miss will have to do." She lowered her eyes to her hands folded on her lap. "Very sorry if that embarrasses you." Her voice was surprisingly soft and well modulated, striking the ear pleasantly. The years of captivity and the slush-mouthed Apache tongue had not dulled its schooled precision.

"The source of embarrassment," the major said quietly, "could be removed, ma'am, given your cooperation."

"No." Her glance came up swiftly, and she was shaking her head. "I'm sorry, but no. I will not even debate the matter, much less consider it. I'm sorry."

Major Kinship sighed and dropped his hands on the desk, palms down. "Why I asked you in has to do with the matter under discussion, Sam." He coughed gently. "Her, ah, the two children—"

"They're mine." Sara Carver's gaze swung to Sam Vetch, and meeting it fully was a little startling. From the moment of her rescue, she had never quite met his eyes or any other man's. That was understandable; but now there was no uncertainty in her, only a rooted and inflexible determination. Without raising her voice, she said again softly, "They're mine," and laid her glance on the major. "I wish that you could understand—but that you cannot doesn't change a thing. They will go with me."

Vetch cleared his throat. "They're with the 'Paches I saw over by the feed sheds?"

"The older boy is," Kinship said. "The baby is with the post surgeon's wife at their quarters. Napping. Little fellow seems a bit sickly—"

"He will be all right," Sara Carver said, "with me."

The major scowled at the backs of his hands. "I was about to say that we could tend the baby here and, when he's a little stronger, send him on to San Carlos and place him with one of the Cherry-cow families. Same for the older boy, but he can leave at once with the others. They are Chiricahua, I imagine?"

"They are my sons," Sara Carver said evenly,

her tone leaving not a jot of room for argument.

Again Kinship sighed. "Perhaps you can talk her out of this foolishness, Sam. Tell her—"

"No," Vetch said.

The major regarded him unhappily. "Did you say no?"

"Her kids are her blood, and that ain't any man's right to say to her." Vetch sat slack in his chair, his long legs outstretched and crossed, eying the toe of one moccasin. He felt Sara Carver's surprised, appraising glance touch him, and meeting it, saw a faint smile bow her chapped lips. He thought idly that despite her dark hair and eyes, she was light-complected under her deep weather stain. He supposed that her face would not be full even if she were less gaunt, and probably she would be on the plain side, though not ill favored—but it was hard to tell.

After a light explosion of his out-sighing breath Major Kinship said dourly, "I see. You're a large help, Sam. Very well, the problem is hardly original with your case, Miss Carver, but I've used up the standard arguments against what you intend. You say that they will go with you—may I ask exactly where?"

Vetch saw the uncertainty again wash like muddy water across her expression. "I hadn't thought on it yet," she said slowly. "I'm not sure."

"Let's see," Kinship prompted in a kindly voice. "You were born in Ohio, raised in a small town. Father and mother deceased, and you hired out for your keep—to a Quaker family?"

"Yes, the Jerrolds. Thomas Jerrold and his wife." She lowered her gaze. "They were childless, and I—was as much daughter as they ever had. Major Kinship." Her eyes lifted defiantly. "I had surely not counted on returning to their roof, even if they would have me."

The major said obliquely, "You became a Quaker, Miss Carver?"

"I did not, although I attended their meetings and became quite sympathetic to their creed and cause. In fact it was my involvement with the Society of Friends that led to my coming West. As you know, the Friends were instrumental in persuading the government to a more lenient policy toward the Indians—"

"I know," Kinship said dryly. "The so-called 'peace policy'—which has succeeded nicely in tying the army's hands when it comes to doing the job Washington sent us out here to do. A typical feat of bureaucratic consistency. I'm sorry—go on, ma'am."

"As part of their program the Friends sent out a number of teacher-missionaries to the Indian reservations. There was always a need, and never enough educated men or women to fill it." Again Sara Carver lowered her eyes to her lap. "I was still quite young, unmarried, and I imagine looking for something like a cause. I had expressed interest, and Mr. Jerrold suggested that my schooling qualified me as a teacher, which profession I had already considered as a living. Why not go West for the Friends in that capacity? It could be arranged."

"For the sake of the red brethren," Kinship murmured in the same tone of dry irony. "Only it was those same brethren that raided your stagecoach around the Arizona-New Mexico line and carried you off."

"No doubt, sir," she said evenly, "you had a reason for raising the matter."

Major Kinship rose and paced to the window, thoughtfully tugging his lower lip between thumb and forefinger. He stared across the blistered parade ground and said without looking around, "Just pitching a penny or two. Have known a few Quakers. Remarkable people. Almost too good for this world." He turned, looking directly at Sara Carver. "I understand your reluctance to throw yourself on the mercy of people to whom you already must feel indebted, and so regret the necessity for asking you to reconsider your objection. But I must do so, if only because frankly I see no other recourse." He raised a hand quickly. "Don't answer at once, but think. You know, as well as anyone, that Quakers taken as a whole are good people in no hypocritical sense of the word. And you will need 'friends' like these, Miss Carver; in light of what you propose, you will need them desperately. People, that is, who can be told your full story and still accept you, and, more important, the children. Almost certainly no other people would do so."

"You make a point impeccably clear, Major." Sara Carver's voice was tight and low, and her head was bent to hide her eyes. "And you choose its target unerringly—a desperate woman. Why varnish that fact—and of course you are right. I know the Jerrolds and I know they will accept the burden. Please don't count me ungrateful." Almost with a visible wrench, she smoothed the hint of acrid bitterness from her voice. "If I may ask you one favor—I should say one more favor. Of course they must be notified in advance, and since I am sure that you are no stranger to composing such messages, I wonder if you might . . ."

With a wry smile the major nodded and, moving back to his desk, took a sheet of stationery from a drawer, sat down and dipped his pen and began to write rapidly. "I will state the simple facts, ungarnished and unequivocal. Enough to prepare them and no more. Distance has a habit of distorting perspective where issues are human ones. The details will take on a less horrendous significance, I think, when you come to discussing them with the Jerrolds personally."

When he had finished writing, Kinship handed her the message to read, saying, "I'll have that telegram sent off at once. We should have a reply in a few days at the outside. If the Jerrolds' response is positive, we'll have you on the stage to Silverton directly."

While she slowly read the compact wording, silently moving her lips, Kinship touched Vetch with a brisk glance. "Sam, you're heading for Silverton. Have you business that's so pressing it can't wait a day or so?"

"Fairly pressing," Vetch said wryly. "I got a hunch, but go on, anyhow."

The major grinned. "If it wouldn't be asking too much, could you postpone your departure? Miss Carver has told me how you've watched out for her and the kids so far—and a lone woman and children should have a safe escort to a hellhole like Silverton. You might continue to make yourself available till you've seen them safely on the first train East."

Vetch gave a dour nod. "Soon as you've signed that message, sign my check too."

The prospective delay was no more than irksome; the real irritant was Sara Carver's study of him, warm and grateful and puzzled, as if she could not fathom why any man should want to do for her now. She stood up, and both men came stiffly to their feet. On her way to the door she halted, facing Vetch, and extended her hand. "I will be in your debt again, I'm afraid."

Vetch said with some gruffness that he was going to Silverton in any case.

"Whatever your reason—thank you." She added a quiet word of gratitude and good-by to the commandant, then went out.

Vetch waited in the outer office while Major Kinship gave his telegrapher the message and signed the scout's check. He and the major exchanged a bit of self-conscious chitchat preliminary to the never-comfortable words of farewell. Then Vetch left, check in his pocket, for the post sutler's to make some needed purchases.

He found himself idly thinking, as he skirted the parade ground, that this Sara Carver was quite a woman. He remembered the hand she had given him, lean and brown and callused, and found himself comparing it to Miss Evangeline Armitage's hand, white and small and dainty. They shared in common only a look of sure competence, but in no like sense. He could not see Sara Carver pouring tea from a silver service any more than he could visualize Miss Vangie grinding corn with a crude *metate*. Miss Vangie's hands were formed for her work, the deft and delicate hand stitching of dresses for Silverton's better class of women. He could see Sara Carver punching spittle-worked hide with an awl for sewing with thongs. The one moved in his mind against a background of rose-patterned walls and scented lace and old china; the other . . .

Uncomfortably Vetch pulled up this thought, as if unwilling to accommodate this scene with its overtones of a white woman's abasement. He was not proud of his mental hedging; it was sugar-coating a fact. Yet he realized that Sara Carver was a woman of tempered fiber. Her thinness from privation was illusory; she was strongly built, and being worked like a draft animal had hardened her sturdy body. But she would need more to survive the Apache woman's frugal lot; as a prisoner, lonely and terrified and abused, she would need to achieve an inner fortitude as tough as rawhide—as flexible too.

Before this he had seen white women who

had lived through Indian captivity. Some of them were beaten into pitiful wrecks. Others refused to return to their old world, some few because they had become utterly Indian in thought and ways, others because they shrank from facing their own people. Only a woman of fiber could survive Apache captivity with her old personality intact, ready at once to take up the threads of a broken past. To shrug away those nine years took courage; to carry their legacy of two copper-skinned children into her new-old life took even more.

A woman deranged from her experience might do so with equanimity; a woman of Sara Carver's calm intelligence could not minimize in her own mind the ordeal that would face her. Without the children she might have dissembled before the world. Instead she had knowingly chosen the way that would brand her in the world's eyes.

Chapter Three

The adobe sprawl of Ocotillo town was an easy walk from the fort, and here at high noon a couple of days later Vetch and the woman and two half-breed boys, aged eight and one, boarded the stage for Silverton.

Accompanying them was Nick Tana, wearing the new suit he had purchased at the sutler's. The ill-fitted slop-shops hampered his lithe movements, and the stiff glossy shoes pinched his feet. But he wore his new derby with the jaunty impudence of youth and despite his limp carried his hand-carved cane with a debonair poise.

They got situated well before the stage was ready to roll, Vetch and Nick sharing one seat. Nick's bad leg was stretched straight out, resting on the seat opposite beside Sara Carver and her eight-year-old, whom she called Jimmie Joe. He had an Apache name that was never breathed aloud because malign spirits could work him ill if they learned it; since he was too young to have earned a spoken name, he was called simply *ish-kay-nay*, a boy. But Sara had given him a secret name; her two brothers Jim and Joe had died in boyhood and to help her mind hold to the details of her past she had named her first son Jimmie Joe; now she used the name aloud and often, with quiet pleasure.

The boy sat solemn and still-faced while Nick Tana gently joshed him in both Apache and English, but he seemed to relax before Nick's friendly manner. Jimmie Joe and Nick Tana were alike, in their veins the blood of two races. True to his breeding, the boy kept Vetch at an arm's length of smoldering reserve, tolerating the white man only because Vetch obviously rated high with his mother and Nick Tana. *Otherwise*, Vetch reflected, *he would be seeing me as buzzard bait every time he looked at me*.

The boy was wearing slightly oversized white boy's jeans and shirt, fresh and stiff-creased from the sutler's shelf, and his black hair had been trimmed in a spruce waterfall. *One day he'll go back to the Apache*, Vetch thought, *when his mother's hold is gone. Jimmie Joe is already too old, but if a man said so she wouldn't hear it*.

Nick Tana grunted and winced, shifting his weight on the seat. "Maybe I should of stayed in that hospital some longer."

"You should have left them dancin' slippers

off anyhow," said Vetch, at slack ease against the horsehair-padded cushions, in his washed but soft-worn scouting clothes. "You need to get perfumed like a Frenchman to get drunk in Silverton?"

"Why"—Nick winked soberly—"I might just look me up some company too. Sam, we ought to tie on one snorter for old times."

Vetch smiled, shaking his head. "Times past, Nick. From here on I look just ahead."

"Well, I sure wish you all the best, you and your lady. Hard to think of us busting up for good. We made a team, Sam."

Vetch said, "You want to come along, Nick, my place could use another hand."

Nick made a wry face. "Ranching ain't for me, but thanks."

"Keep it in mind anyhow. Soledad County, New Mexico. My place is twenty miles east of Spanish Crossing if you change your mind or ever come drifting."

The driver was clambering to his high seat, the coach rocking on its thorough braces. At the last moment, as he kicked off the brake, a man called, "Hold on!" and wrenched open the stage door and climbed in, sandwiching himself between Vetch and Nick Tana.

The belated passenger was a talker, and, from the thick burly set of his body in a cheap checked suit, might have been a prize fighter, but his black sample case was the badge of the drummer. "Reed Toomey," he said, flashing a yellow grin. "Your pleasure, gents." He opened the bag, displaying a selection of miniature sample bottles. "Old Crow, J. H. Cutter, Mountain Brook—will you sweeten the dust with me?"

Vetch declined, wedged roughly against the side panel by Toomey's considerable bulk. Nick accepted a whisky sample. Toomey drained his bottle—"Ahhh!"—and lowered it, his bloodshot and benign gaze falling on Jimmie Joe. "How you there, sonny? Nice-looking boy. Kind o' thin. He yours, missus?"

"Yes."

"Nice-looking boy. Pretty dark, ain't he? Say-y-y—" Toomey leaned forward, chuckling. "Oh, he surely is dark. That baby likewise. Why, lady, I do vow—"

"Good thing if a man keeps his mouth closed when the stage is movin'," Vetch said. "Dust is hell this time of year."

Toomey showed a raffish, veiled grin. "Yeah." His tone was deeply amused. "Well, don't that beat all."

The stage rolled west into the deepening afternoon. The lemon-colored sunlight beat with a brassy fury against the panels and dust curtains, the heat wearing through them. The interior of the coach was close and suffocating; the alkali that filtered through every opening and crack was bitter to breathe and taste, and it powdered every surface exposed to it. The baby began slowly to cough, deep retching coughs that made a man uneasy.

Sara Carver tugged her frayed shawl around

the infant's mouth and held her own face close to his as if breathing for him, faintly crooning to him, whether in Apache or English, Vetch could not tell. He was a puny little one for certain. The tyke's white blood and the lean Apache fare might have mixed badly, that was all, and he only wanted fattening.

Vetch took the opportunity, while the woman's face was averted, to give her a frank and curious study. With the probity of a direct mind, he saw why those nine years, while marking her in subtle ways, had failed to touch the essential Sara Carver. She lived in that rare grace of self that could preserve its identity intact through any ordeal, any disruption of its existence, because, self-contained, it did not depend on outward props to shore it up.

Even so, it was not immune to outside thrusts; he had seen a flush stain her dark thin cheeks at Toomey's sly observations. Her breeding and upbringing had been gentle; even these nine years could not eradicate the moral habits of that upbringing, and now that she faced a return to the atmosphere of morality the opinions of the many, righteous and unrighteous, could not fail to touch her.

Toomey's words had provided a sampling of what would come, and Vetch wondered if even a woman like this one could stand the gaff. If she were uncompromisingly to accept it on her own account, she could not ignore the fact of her action's placing a like burden on the two young lives in her care. Vetch hadn't considered that aspect of the matter before, and now he wondered. If misgivings later came to Sara Carver, they would probably not be for herself. And if she faltered then—what? Time alone could give the answer.

The afternoon wore on and was spent. The land lost its barren glitter, and a tan twilight puddled along rock formations and etched them with lean veined shadows; twilight tenderly swaddled a line of wind-ribbed dunes on the near horizon. The light and the heat dropped off tolerably, but the landscape remained strongly defined, and a vagrant sigh of wind was like a warm breath.

As swift dusk came the squat outlines of the Henery station grew out of the desert floor, its 'dobe house and sheds and ratty tangle of ocotillo pole corrals less squalid with the muting of coming night. The driver braked up, the wheels sliding in a cloud of moiling dust. Dace Henery, a bald tub of a man wearing checked pants supported by bright red galluses, wheezed out with a lantern and stood garrulously by while the passengers dropped stiffly to the ground. The Mexican hostler set to unhitching the six horses as Henery led the way inside.

They sat at a trestle table in the low smoky room and were served watery beans, stringy beef, and coffee that would pass the floating-nail test. The food was brought by the widowed Henery's daughter, a tow-headed girl of fifteen who went barefoot and was embarrassingly womanly under her drab sack of a dress. Henery half filled four tin cups with pale liquor at his plank bar, diluted it to a drinkable ratio from the water bucket by the door, and carried the cups to the table, setting one in front of each man, including the driver.

"She's the ole white mule, boys. You drink up. You won't find nothing like that in Silverton." He poured a cup for himself, not adding water, and sat at the foot of the table, folding his fat, soft arms on it. "You boys heard what happened at the Stack ranch down below the Gila? Reckon not; you come from the wrong direction. Well, the word will get around quick enough hereafter, you mark me."

The driver said, "You mind turning off long enough a man can ask what you're running on about?"

"Got the word this morning from the driver on the eastbound run. Stack fambly is been wiped out." Henery paused impressively. "Uncle Billy Stack and his wife and their boy Arno. The talk is that it was a pret' ugly thing."

"Wiped out?" Reed Toomey arrested a forkful of beans short of his mouth. "You mean Indians, eh?"

The driver said sharply, " 'Pache? They ain't out in no force these days. The army cornered Nachita and Loco, and Toriano's bunch too, up hard by Fort Thomas. Ask Sam Vetch here and Nick Tana; they scouted for the detail that brought in Toriano's women and young ones. If any more busted from San Carlos, why ain't there been word out?"

"Didn't say this was 'Pache work." Henery paused meditatively and drained his cup. He smacked his lips and returned to the bar, this time bringing the jug to the table. "Uncle Billy, he was laying in the doorway with his head pret' near blowed away. Looked like a long-range gun with an expandin' slug done the job. His wife was inside on the floor, and she was knifed three, four times. Arno, he was shot clean through the chest at close range." Henery paused, tapping his cup with a fingernail to stress each word. "Now you tell me, boys. Looked like Arno and the old woman was taken live for sure. You heard of 'Paches taking folks live to kill them clean?"

"Not likely," the driver said. " 'Paches will mutilate a dead body, not to say a live. They don't cotton to watching a live one die fast."

Nick Tana, who was listening attentively, frowning, said, "How you know it was Injun?"

"They was scalped," Henery said with a sage nod, "all three."

"That's maybe Injun," Nick said, "but not 'Pache. Man, anyone can take a scalp. The governor of Sonora put a bounty on 'Pache scalps, and the Mexes—Americans too—collected on them."

"No need for your red dander," the station owner growled. "I said the sign wa'n't 'Pache on the face of her. But the place was combed over fine by who done it, and nothing taken but maybe a little grub. Seemed to be searching after something, but not money, for Uncle Billy had a wad of greenbacks hid and it was left scattered on the floor. I call that Injun. So is poisoning a well with a man's body," he added in afterthought. "Arno got dumped in the well."

Nick nodded reluctantly, scowling at the table, but it was a scowl of perplexity more than anything.

Vetch broke the brief silence. "How many of them? Any idea?"

"Now there is a caution. Deputy sheriff at Silverton went over the ground with a Pima tracker. Damn' little sign, and that pointed Injun. A fella had crouched out in the brush to get Uncle Billy and there was barefoot pony track alongside there. This fella don't make but a little moccasin sign." Henery paused again, lifted a stubby finger and waggled it. "One horse, one rifle, and one man. If it make sense, this red son must of been on a one-man war sortie."

Nick Tana raised his head quickly then, and there was a sharp yet nearly inaudible whisper—"*Salvaje*"—but it did not come from the half-breed.

Sara Carver was sitting at the foot of the table, head bent while she coaxed the baby to drink a little of the fresh milk provided by the Henery cow. Close to her elbow, Jimmie Joe struggled inefficiently with the knife and fork his mother had enjoined him to use. He understood no English or very little, but as the single whispered word left his mother now, he sat bolt

49

upright, his black eyes shining on her face.

The boy said a word or two in Apache, very softly, and Sara silenced him in the same tongue, and sharply. Her glance shuttled once around the table, and she stood then and moved slowly toward the door, rocking the baby in her arms. The boy followed her outside, noiseless as a shadow.

Vetch glanced at Nick Tana, who was staring after the three of them, a thoughtful scowl on his face. Vetch felt a puzzlement of his own; *salvaje* was the Spanish for "savage," a word that as an adjective could apply to the atrocity Henery had just described. It was also a proper noun. The word coming from Sara Carver in a startled whisper, and her furtive manner afterward, made an uneasy riddle.

Henery and the driver apparently had not caught this brief byplay, and Toomey was now occupied in teasing Henery's daughter and evoking fits of wild giggling from her. "Henery, it's a plenty big puzzle, sure as you're a liar," the driver was saying as Vetch rose and walked to the doorway.

The dusk was like a dusty curtain flung across the sleeping desert; the shapes of ancient ridges and rocks blurred into a beige-gray anonymity. Toward the deep east a colorless moon swam behind tattered veils of cloud. A short distance from the 'dobe the woman paced slowly up and down in the silent dust of the road, crooning to the baby; she made a skirted and indistinct form. Her son paced behind her, putting his feet in her shoe marks. Presently he tired of the game and moved off to squat by the tall hump of an anthill, his head bent over it.

Vetch paused to fumble out a cigar and a match, then sauntered across the yard; he snapped the match alight on a thumbnail and drew the cigar to life as he halted by the road. Sara Carver came to a motionless stop yards away, her face turned to him, waiting.

"Fine night."

She began to pace again and after a dozen steps she said, "As good as any, I suppose. You see so many and they all run together in your mind."

"They're alike," Vetch said. "Different too. It depends on how a body looks at things. Would reckon you have had your crawful of this country by day or night."

She halted again; she murmured to the baby, who was mildly fretful, then said, "No, that's not it. You get used to the country after a bit, and when you get over being frightened, things like the sun and the moon, even a tree or creek, can seem like friends. When you're a prisoner, a slave, trying to remember what freedom was like—these things come to represent freedom for you."

"You had a lonely time of it. That the hardest part?"

"No. I mean yes, for a while, till the land itself no longer seemed hostile. Then I used every opportunity to get off by myself, as now. I suppose I'm spoiled for human company for good." Her teeth made a lighter dimness, smiling, in the lowering night. "Otherwise there's much to what you suggest. There was little to tempt me in the human company available. When your cavalry caught up with us the woman who ran after me with a knife—do you remember?"

Vetch gave a bleak nod. "Ought to. First woman I ever shot."

"You only wounded her in the arm. And saved my life. Make no mistake, she meant to kill me." Sara's voice dropped almost to a whisper. "She swore that if my own people ever found me she would kill me. Until then she would bide her time. She hated me—I never thought that anyone, even an Apache, could contain so much hatred."

"Who was she?"

"Neeta. His—other wife."

Vetch was silent for a full ten seconds, digesting the revelation. Major Kinship had mentioned to him how, when the C.O. had questioned her about the Indian who had sired her children, intending to see that the two boys were united with their father when he was taken, she had been evasive, giving only a stony answer or two that made no sense. Still, that she might be sensitive and enigmatic on this matter was understandable; it was a chapter in her life that she could only wish to forget.

Mention of the "other wife" was the first hint she had given of her situation during captivity, and he said tentatively, "You were married, then."

"Surely. In the Apache manner, of course—"

"Not unheard of," Vetch said. "Unusual, though. The man. He went on ahead with Toriano when the men split off from you?"

She was silent for a moment. "Immediately after wounding Neeta you shot a man who came at you with a lance. You shot him fatally."

Vetch nodded. "Sergeant Rudabaugh fired same time. Might have been his bullet, mine, or both that finished him. . . ." The last words trailed off as dawning comprehension flooded him, and then he said foolishly, "The man?"

"Perhaps I should have said so before," she murmured. "But you've been kind to me—to us. I did not want you to feel bad because of—if you do feel so. Believe me, you have no reason to. Does that sound callous?"

Vetch said, "I guess not," but thinking on it then, found the situation strange enough, chatting almost casually with a woman about how he had shot the father of her children. Automatically his glance found Jimmie Joe, who was demolishing the anthill in deadly earnest.

"He doesn't know," Sara Carver said quietly. "He can't understand what we're saying, and I told him only that his father was killed in the fight. I would not want him to hate the man who helped us."

Vetch ducked his head, staring at the cigar going dead between his fingers. He made no move to relight it, and after an onrunning silence he said, "It's been a hard time for you. Down in Mexico all these years I reckon you had no chance to be found or get away."

"None, till now. Toriano had a stronghold in the Sierra Madre, and he left it only to raid. If the Mexican army had not finally chased him across the border I might have lived out my life among the Apaches—and I'm not altogether sure that I am wise in electing not to." It was the first suggestion of bitterness he had heard, perhaps because their meager talk heretofore had not invited confidence. "You know, I practically forced Major Kinship to give me the children by threatening to stay with the tribe. And it was almost a decision, Mr. Vetch, not simply a threat."

"Reckon I understand. But you could face a sight worse."

"You mean thanks be to the Jerrolds that I am not forced to. In extenuation, I did form my final choice before the major made his suggestion concerning them."

"Must be a rare kind of people."

Sara Carver's chin came up slightly. "Because they are willing to take back an Indian's leavings, you mean?"

"No, ma'am, I do not."

The baby gave a broken, coughing wail; she patted him and sighed, "I know, you're tired," afterward looking directly at the ex-scout. "I realize that, Mr. Vetch, and I do apologize. Worry does not improve the temper."

"Worried about these Jerrolds?"

"People can change a great deal in nine years. I was a girl of nineteen when the Apaches took me." Again the bitterness filled her voice; she said, "I am no longer a girl, and that is a small part of what I no longer am. And I cannot be insensible to the burden I will place on them, their ready acceptance notwithstanding."

"There's times," Vetch said slowly, "when there ain't a choice, saving maybe two bad ones. You put your money on the wheel and let her spin, hoping for the lesser evil, I reckon. All a body can do then is wait and see."

"On the wheel—" She hesitated. "A gambling term, sir?"

"Yes'm."

"I am afraid that I am no longer shocked by such expressions; Indians, you know, are inveterate gamblers." She studied him strangely. "You are a rare kind of person yourself. I can understand one who is prompted to think and do right from a sense of religious duty, but I think that's not the case with you—and yet—" She smiled a little, shaking her head. "I really don't understand you—a rough, unfeeling frontiersman."

The gentle irony, as well as the compliment, was embarrassing to Vetch; he looked uneasily over her head. How could you answer a question about what drove you when you were sure of no such answer as folks usually gave? People had too many pat solutions to the big questions for which there might well be no answers that lay within man's comprehension. All he felt with any fair degree of certainty was that in living close to the earth, to wild things free of sham or pretense, he had found his own bed-rock. He knew his flaws as a man, as he knew equally well the things that preyed on those flaws. Similarly he had found that what was good in him responded to such goodness as it encountered in living. As Miss Vangie Armitage could bring out his gentleness in one way, so did Sara Carver and her pathetic situation in another way.

The silver disk of the moon had gained intensity with first darkness, and now it bathed the rugged land in a cruel relief of bright and black, like the face of a dead world. A cool wind feathered off the ridges, and Sara Carver pulled the worn shawl tighter about her shoulders. "A cast-off shawl and a cast-off woman—how naturally they go together. Do we leave here soon?"

"Soon enough." His voice was gruff. "Thing to do is push all that away, what's past."

"Why?"

Vetch glanced at the boy Jimmie Joe, and tipped his head toward the baby. That was all.

"Their sake, if not for mine. Very reasonable, Mr. Vetch. If I only can." She moved past him toward the house. After a few steps she looked back and said, "Thank you," almost primly, then entered the building.

Vetch relighted his cigar and walked up the road a short distance, unlimbering his stiff joints. When he came back to the station the Mexican hostler was hitching the fresh teams to the coach. Henery exited from the building, lantern swinging in his fist, and lighted the passengers' way to the stage.

Nick Tana split off from the others and walked to meet Vetch, who halted as Nick came up. He said, low-voiced, "No mix of mine, Sam, but she tell you anything about her 'Pache husband?"

Vetch thought, *Now that's odd*, and eyed him quizzically. "Said he was the buck me and Rudabaugh shot. Maybe you knew that, Nick?"

"Me?" Nick Tana scrubbed a palm over his neck, shaking his head. "Nope. I didn't know." He seemed to hesitate, then said abruptly, "Let's get on," and headed for the coach.

now I want to hear the—"

Kate suddenly stood. The crack and boom of thunder shook the window. "We're getting out of here," Jo shouted. "Come on, Kate. I'll get you out of here while Dan Bailey runs—"

"What in the devil do you want?" said a deep, unfamiliar voice from the back of the car.

"Jesus H. Christ," said Jo, "who are you?"

"Name is Vince Strudlick, a state trooper," the man said. "And you, I didn't know. It's a state trooper," Jo said abruptly. "Come on," said Jo and headed for the car.

Chapter Four

The stage rolled through the long darkness till the stars faded and the sky paled in the east. The light grew steadily, and it was full dawn when they made a fifteen-minute change stop and had a hasty breakfast. At midmorning they came into Silverton.

It was a mining town, surging and savage and opulent, and the first sight of it after a long absence always gave Vetch a remote shock. He had a taste for still and lonely reaches, and here the din and turmoil rolled at a man from all sides like roaring waves, hammering and numbing his senses. On the flats a distance below Silverton, the ore-reduction mills made their incessant racket by day and night; coming into the lower town, the passengers were engulfed by a dense traffic of the big ore wagons that shuttled back and forth between the mills and the silver mines scattered on the mountain slopes above. The stage driver had to fight his way through the wagons, giving their teamsters curse for blistering curse. Miners of a polyglot of nationalities swarmed the sidewalks; rigs and saddle horses overflowed the tie rails of the long four blocks of the main street. Every other building, ranging from canvas tents to raw new false fronts and an occasional brick building, was a saloon or gambling den. A humming excitement overlaid the whole bedlam of Silverton, for it was a boom town in its prime, attracting hangers-on and camp followers from every corner of the West, and with them the swindling and drinking and brawling, the shootings and the knifings.

The driver braked to a stop by the Monarch Hotel, and his passengers descended, dusty and beaten from their day and night of sheer punishment. Nick Tana was eager to begin his rounds of Silverton's delights, and, limping away, he lost himself in the throng.

Vetch walked to the rear boot where the driver was digging out Reed Toomey's valise. He passed it to the burly drummer, then handed Vetch his slender war bag. "All the best, Sam."

"Thanks, Toby." He tramped up the hotel steps, shouldering through the loungers standing about on the porch. Sara Carver clung instinctively to his arm, and Jimmie Joe hugged her skirt, demoralized by his first sight of a white man's boom town.

The Stalking Moon

The lobby of the Monarch had some pretensions of elegance, with its elaborate chandelier and deep red carpet now sadly dilapidated by countless muddy boots. Vetch crossed to the desk, dropping his war bag on it. The balding clerk turned from sorting mail in the pigeon-hole rack, recognizing him at once. "Mr. Vetch. Good to have you back, sir. The room you like is vacant, rear one on the southeast corner."

"Room for the lady too," Vetch said. "One next to mine if it ain't taken."

"Certainly," the clerk began, turning the register book toward him and reaching for the pen. His hand froze, and he raised his eyes very slowly. "Ah, Mr. Vetch—"

Vetch conceded a few words of explanation. "I'm escorting the lady from Fort Sutro. I am looking out for her till she takes the train East."

"Of course," the clerk said carefully. "These— those two children. Am I mistaken, or—"

"No."

"I'm sorry. I do not make hotel policy." The clerk's voice began to fray as Vetch simply looked at him, and he started to fidget. He let his gaze fall to the register. "We don't want trouble, sir. Please."

"No trouble," Vetch said. "I'll sign for us all, you give me the two keys, and we'll go upstairs nice and quiet. No trouble at all." His tone held an easy suggestion that the clerk could have all he wanted.

The clerk's lips twisted on the edge of more speech; he thought better of it and handed

Vetch the pen with a limp hand. Vetch signed and paid him, and headed for the landing. As they went up the stairs Sara Carver murmured, "That is part of what I must get used to, I suppose."

"Yes, ma'am," Vetch said tonelessly, and could not help adding, "Hope you did not expect better."

"No. I realize that it could be worse—I was thinking of the boys."

Now it begins, Vetch thought. The seed of knowledge that would grow in her, perhaps until it mushroomed into an unsupportable guilt. There were at least two sides to any question; there were sound arguments for not leaving her children on a savage and sterile reservation, but from now on her conscience would listen increasingly to the other side. The insights and judgments that came easily even while he could never phrase them aloud irritated Vetch. *None of your damn business. How come you can't settle your mind to that?*

In the corridor Vetch paused by his door, handing her the key to the adjoining room. "You clean up, ma'am, and get some rest. That little 'un can stand all the sleep he can get. I will check on the next eastbound train, and meantime I won't be far away."

Sara Carver extended her hand, and he felt its warmth and strength. "Mr. Vetch, how can I thank you enough? It is time I asked that question, I think."

"That says it all, ma'am. You get some rest."

The Stalking Moon

Vetch unlocked his room and went in, dumping the contents of his war bag on the bed. An enlisted man's wife at Fort Sutro who took in laundry had cleaned his single suit during his absence on patrol. Tucking the rolled black broadcloth under his arm, he left his room and the hotel and sought the nearest barbershop. After a shave and haircut he entered the bathhouse at the rear and soaked for a half hour in a big wooden barrel, directing the aged attendant who polished his boots to keep the bath at scalding point with pails of boiling water.

As he left the shop, a little stiff in his clean, slightly wrinkled suit, he almost collided with Nick Tana. Nick had been drinking. He leaned a straight arm on Vetch's shoulder, waggling a finger in his face with careful gravity. "I know a Mex gal who keeps house for the quality on the hill." He made a sweeping gesture toward the row of big houses on the slope backing the town, homes of merchants and mine owners. "I am heading for to see her, but first I make tall medicine with you, chief. We catchem firewater and powwow."

"Later. I'm on your sort of errand myself, and I don't aim to call on a lady smelling like a busted bung."

"You can chew on cloves after," Nick Tana said. "I'd like some powwow, Sam."

His dark young face was suddenly serious, and though Vetch knew that Nick's moods when he had been drinking were mercurial and usually illogical, he sensed something here that gave him pause. Pulling his old watch from his vest, he saw that it was still an hour till noon, and Miss Vangie Armitage would be busy with the forenoon swell of business at her little shop.

He said, "Let's have a drink, Nick," and the two of them quartered across to the Nugget Saloon. The long room was only thinly crowded at this hour, with a trace of yesterday's tainted air, but still holding the pleasant coolness of morning.

Nick hiked his heel over the brass rail. "We'll have a bottle, Jack," he told the bartender. Vetch rubbed a hand over his mouth to cover a grin, since this was how Nick addressed all strange white men.

"We don't serve Injuns."

"Look again."

The bartender did, carefully, and said, "Or breeds."

"You can serve the white half," Nick said agreeably, "and kick the other half out any time you want to try, Jack." Only his lips grinned, and without a word the bartender brought the bottle. Nick said to Vetch, "He's an observant man. You can tell he is," as he palmed the bottle. He scooped up two glasses from an inverted row of them on the bar and moved to a table deep in a back corner. Vetch toed out a chair and sat, characteristically stretching his legs and thumbing back his hat. Nick lifted his brows as he poured their drinks. "Any trouble getting 'em into that fleabag the Monarch? The kids, I mean?"

"Clerk felt troublesome," Vetch said. "He got religion all right."

Nick chuckled, lifted his glass in mild salute, drank, and slung an arm over the back of his chair. "Sam, you ever hear of a 'Pache called Ya-ik-tee?"

Vetch thought a moment; he tossed off his drink before replying. "Strikes a chord, nothing to put my finger on. Let's see. *Ya-ik-tee* means 'dead,' don't it, or 'death'?"

"Hell," Nick said, "you know there is no changing 'Pache names to English. Nearest you can put it in English is, 'He is not present,' which is to say, polite as hell, 'He is dead.'"

"How did a man come by a name like that?"

"'Pache earns his name. Ya-ik-tee earned his by being strange. No other word for it. People living in tribes do everything together, Sam—only way to survive. Food is a common property; if one starves, all do. Hard for them to understand why a man would split off alone. This Ya-ik-tee has always gone it that way. Toriano's band is as much folks as he ever admitted to, and even they see him damn seldom. Still he's a great warrior, maybe the greatest in the Apache nation."

"Seems I've heard a story or two. The lone Apache—always let it pass as an old wives' tale."

"This side of the border them stories sound like moonshine. But down in Sonora where they know He-Is-Dead in the flesh, he is damn real. The Mexes down there call him by a name of their own—Salvaje."

Vetch had been listening with idle interest, and now he came abruptly alert. Nick nodded a wry acknowledgment of the name's significance, and then went on. "There is a radius of a good hundred miles there where the Mexes tell their kids if they ain't good, Salvaje will get them. It ain't stretching things to say the 'Paches themselves are scared of him. It's said he has no religion but killing Mexes, so it follows his own personal medicine must be damn strong. From that a notion got started that he was killed once and can't be killed again. They count him as more than human—not one of them—*tatsan*."

Nick paused, refilling their glasses, and Vetch murmured, "Go on."

"You remember old Henery telling us about them three people killed by a lone Injun? Two of 'em taken alive and not tortured—but scalped? There's only one lone hunter kills like that: Salvaje. Maybe he was away when Toriano left the Madre and struck out north. He could be following Toriano now, leaving his peculiar trail."

Vetch shook his head. "I don't get this, Nick. You driving at something?"

Nick hunched forward, leaning his crossed arms on the table, lowering his voice almost to a murmur. "I never seen Salvaje—or Ya-iktee—and there ain't a lot of people outside Toriano's bunch that have, short of plenty dead Mexicans. I am just telling you what's common knowledge among my ma's people. And here's something else I heard that's common talk. That Salvaje's wife is a white woman who lives with Toriano's people."

Vetch was silent for a moment, scowling. "You know there was only one white woman found with his bunch."

"Sure." Nick nodded, his eyes speculative. "You saw how her and the kid reacted when Henery was talking. She even said the name, Salvaje. Then the kid started to talk up and she cut him off." He paused, then added pointedly, "But she told you her 'Pache husband was the man Sarge Rudabaugh and you shot. What do you make of that, Sam?"

Vetch revolved his empty glass between his fingers. "That could just be her affair, Nick, and nobody else's."

Nick shrugged. "None of mine, for sure. I ain't so certain about you. Anyhow, I figured you should be told."

"Why?"

"That Carver woman looks up to you. She needs a man to look up to and she has settled on you."

"That has a pretty wild sound."

"I see it as natural. You have stuck by her and helped her from the day we found her."

"You know why," Vetch said irritably. "What else could a man do?"

"I know, but she is bound to have a feeling about it. Gives you an interest in her, sort of, so I reckoned—"

"Look," Vetch said flatly. "Whether she told

me the truth or not, for whatever reason, it ain't mix of mine. I don't even make the matter important."

"Maybe you're right."

"Just maybe." Vetch came to his feet, spinning a coin on the table to pay for his share of the bottle, which Nick would drink. "Didn't mean to sound rough. Appreciate the thought, Nick."

Nick nodded lazily, lifting a palm in a semicircling gesture. "See you later, chief."

Chapter Five

Leaving the Nugget, Vetch headed uptown. Because it was payday at the mines the town was achieving at an early hour the roistering and feverish pace, latent with violence, that usually began in late afternoon. Today's first-shift miners had quit work and were trickling into town. Vetch breasted solid bunches of them, Mexicans, Poles, Swedes, Germans, Welsh and Cornish and Irish, divided by their ancient, truculent nationalisms and spoiling to release cumulative tensions.

Vetch had the passing thought that hell would break loose before sundown; otherwise he took bare notice of the savage zest keening to life around him, in which at odd times he had taken a man's rough and primal pleasure. He found himself turning over in his mind the possibility that Sara Carver might calmly have lied to him concerning her late Apache husband, finding himself strangely nettled by that likelihood. Yet what reason could she have for lying? *And supposing she is, what can you do about it?*

Doggedly he shook away these thoughts and put his attention on the small ordeal that faced him immediately.

The boiling traffic of the lower town cooled to a sedate crawl as he crossed into the respectable business section, as if an invisible line had been drawn across Silverton's north end between the lawless and the orderly. The handful of saloons and gambling halls here were plush and expensively furnished, catering to a moneyed and well-behaved clientele.

He halted by a small shop with the gilded letters DRESSES AND MILLINERY MADE TO ORDER across its window, nervously adjusting his tie, giving the instep of each boot a furtive rub along his pants legs. An unexpected panic took hold of him, and he had the impulse to head for the nearest saloon. Resolutely he put it down, palmed open the door and tramped inside.

Chatting with a customer, Miss Vangie Armitage did not at once notice him. Vetch stood just within the doorway, turning his hat between his hands, which felt inordinately large and awkward. He ran a nervous glance around the shop. The long cutting table with its remnants of dress goods, the newfangled sewing machine and several dressmakers' dummies and a stack of hatboxes on a counter framed a feminine, totally alien setting that by itself always made him uneasy.

The customer turned to leave, Miss Vangie saying, "Call again, Mrs. Thatcher," and then her gaze found Vetch and sparkled with a surprised pleasure. "Why, Sam Vetch! I certainly hadn't expected to see you again so soon."

Vetch waited till the sharp-nosed Mrs. Thatcher had reluctantly gone; he moved forward and took her hand, bowing stiffly above it. "Miss Vangie, it is surely good to see you, ma'am."

"Why, I do thank you, sir." She dropped a little curtsy and laughed, but she was always pleased by his manner, that of a shy and respectful man, one properly raised yet little accustomed to women.

Miss Vangie Armitage was a small woman, at thirty-two edging toward a matronly buxomness that did not detract from the trim fullness of her figure. Her face was softly round, placid and sweet in its frame of smooth black hair drawn back in a plum-tight bun. There was about her a subdued and gentle air, except for her dress of blue moire, expensive and finely cut to advertise her trade. The dress and a pair of tiny turquoise earrings flattered her vivid eyes.

"Sam, I—I *am* glad to see you." She tilted her head with a faint smile, as if the thought surprised her a little. "And you've finished your last job for the army—you are going to your ranch in New Mexico?"

"Yes'm." Vetch cleared his throat. "Miss Vangie—"

"Have you eaten this noon?"

Vetch lied that he had, his stomach in no state for food, and she said, "At least you'll have a cup of tea while I eat. Come along." She led the way to the rear of the shop, overriding his protest. "My goodness, it's broad daylight and surely I can invite a gentleman to tea without setting Mrs. Thatcher's tongue clacking."

They entered a spacious kitchen-living room that was simply furnished, yet immaculate in its prim gentility, as if the entire room and its contents had been lifted intact from a more likely setting and laid incongruously down in Silverton. In its homelier details it was not unlike a ranch or farm common room anywhere, with its big iron stove and sink with pump, a circular dining table with four chairs, and a leather-covered settee and armchair. Its highly personalized aspects lay in the fine oaken highboy and shelves with a tasteful display of china dishes and elaborate gimcracks that he supposed were cherished heirlooms.

Vetch gingerly took the chair she indicated. He watched her move briskly between the stove and table, preparing sandwiches and tea, and slowly the grinding tensions of the past days slipped from him. As always the orderly peace of this room made the violent world outside seem remote and unreal. In this room he had first felt the formless, unvoiced yearnings that brought with them the painful nostalgia of boyhood memories, of a Virginia farm home and a genteel and gracious mother. The sense of something missing had left an empty ache, and suddenly he had known an overwhelming conviction of what he wanted.

He had met Miss Vangie Armitage a good ten months ago, when he had seen her caught on the sidewalk in a surge of drunken miners. With his glimpse of her pale face in the melee, Vetch had plowed his way to her side and escorted her safely to her doorstep, where he had accepted her offer of tea. Afterward, weaving his dreams and looking forward to each subsequent visit, he had failed to push a formal courtship.

Sam Vetch's proper training had ceased at sixteen, when he had fled home after killing two Yankee soldiers who came foraging for food on their farm while his father and brothers were at war. That was in the summer of '62 when McClellan was advancing on Richmond and the downfall of the Confederacy had seemed imminent. Faced with the possibility of being hunted as a murderer by an occupation army, he had run far and fast. It was years before he could safely consider returning, and somehow never got around to it. There had been no time of young courtship in his life; now fumbling and overcautious in his inexperience, he had pressed no suit with the woman he had settled on.

Miss Vangie served tea and he found himself watching her hands, white and small, yes, but brisk and capable at a woman's work, and he thought, *What the hell, a man should chop the wood and fetch the water*, and so thinking, not daring to think more since he might never get the words out, blurted, "Miss Vangie, with your leave, I have got something to say."

Her hand paused holding the teapot over his cup, and she raised her brows. "Yes?"

"I wonder—that is, would you go with me to New Mexico?"

"Sir?"

It was coming out with a wrong and stupid sound, and he swallowed and mustered his words carefully and then spoke them. Afterward he stared into his cup, waiting till she said softly, "Sam," and he looked up, seeing in her face something tender and vulnerable that he had not seen before.

She was smiling with gentle reproach, a soft rose stain in her cheeks. "It is a sudden thing, Sam."

"No, Miss Vangie, it ain't. I hardly know how to say it, but it is no way sudden, believe me." His hands shook enough to chatter the cup in its saucer, and he set them carefully aside and folded his hands on the table. "I have thought mighty strong on the matter since you—ah, been alone in the world." He meant since her invalid father had died five months ago. "And I—I even readied the house on my ranch like I thought a woman would want, freighting in costly things from Santa Fe, keeping in mind what you told me about your home in New York."

"I see." She moved to the stove, her face turned away, and was silent for so long that he feared he had offended. Then with a depth of smothered emotion that startled him, she said quietly, "I am honored. Deeply honored, but—"

"Miss Vangie, I have a fair education if that's what is troubling you. I know I don't sound it, but the way I have lived—"

"Sam, Sam." She came quickly around with a deprecating gesture. "That isn't it. Any woman should be proud to have you, and as you are, not wanting to change you in the least—unless she were an utter fool." Her hands smoothed her skirt with a quick fluttering motion. "It's not you, Sam, it's me. Or me—and the country. I am afraid that the mixture is a poor one."

There was a faint drift of shouts from the street, and then the crash of a gunshot. Miss Vangie started at the sounds; she gripped the back of a chair, some of the color leaving her face. "It's like that all the time lately—I have forgotten what it is to sleep soundly." She looked straight at him. "Sam, you know that I left the East with my father only because every physician consulted agreed that the dry desert air should have a salutary effect on his health. And because we had to live somehow, I built up this small business in Silverton. After Father died I remained here because I needed to save enough money to return East and start all over. I have nearly enough."

"Miss Vangie, maybe it is just this town and all."

"No. It's the country—this rough, hateful country. The town, the people, merely reflect the total environment. Sam, these people are descended from an orderly, law-abiding race, and in a couple of generations or less they have wiped out over two thousand years of civilized culture! They have degenerated into savages little better than those from which they wrestled the land. The few good men like yourself are a handful of sound kernels amid the dross—"

"Miss Vangie, it won't always be like this. The family men, the settlers will have their day soon and the country will quiet down."

"Don't tell me of what will be—I am thinking of what is. How long do we wait for it, Sam? Ten years? Twenty?"

Vetch tried again, feeling a tenuous desperation crowding him. He had been aware of her longing for the tranquil, ordered life she had known in a small New York village, but had not realized the deepset vehemence of that longing. "My ranch ain't like this desert. It is mighty beautiful country there, mountains and big trees and clean streams. There ain't no people about, so no fighting or shooting, and the only Injuns you'll see are a few drifting, peaceable families that trap and hunt in the high country." Vetch paused, weighing the negations that must be admitted. "It will be a hard life some ways, and mighty lonesome."

She sank slowly into a chair, watching him, and her eyes seemed indrawn and musing now. "I have always worked hard—at cooking and

76

sewing and housekeeping—and I like solitude," she murmured. "Perhaps too well."

His spirit began to lift. "Ma'am, I want you to see the land as I see it now, as well as what it will someday be." He paused, considering, and said with a quiet surprise at his conclusion, "I reckon I could never abide living anywhere else but that place of mine, now."

"I can't picture you elsewhere—somehow it would not be right. Your voice, your whole manner, say it." Her smile was warm and quick, lighting up her small still face. "I am sure of you, Sam, as much as I am unsure of myself. Perhaps I can learn to see the country as you do. But I must think, and I would like a little time, please."

"All you need," Vetch said, and came to his feet, awkwardly fingering his hat. "May I see you tonight?"

"I'll be working rather late, finishing a dress for Mrs. Thatcher. Could you call about seven?" She rose too, laying a hand on his arm. "Thank you, Sam. No matter how I decide, remember that—that nothing could have pleased me more than your asking."

Chapter Six

Leaving the store, Vetch tramped back toward the hotel, his head so full of light musings that the savage curse of a teamster whose loaded wagon just missed him went unheeded. He took only bare notice of the knot of overalled miners standing by the hotel porch, till a burst of jocular laughter left them and a small form spun out from their midst and sprawled in the dust.

It was Jimmie Joe, and instantly he was on his feet, lunging back at the object of his wrath. This was a bear-huge miner, swarthy and kettle-gutted, who slapped his thigh and roared his mirth; a light cuff of his big paw sent the boy into the dust again. This time Jimmie Joe came to his feet more slowly, his jeans and shirt colorless with dust, as if he had already been knocked down a half-dozen times.

"Is great joke, eh," boomed the big miner in the thick accents of a Slovak. "I only say who is the small siwash belonging to and he come at me. Is crazy little Injun, eh?"

The other miners laughed; one of them said, "You look to your scalp, George. He is fixing for the warpath again."

The boy did not stir, but his light wiry body was crouched and set in a wrestler's stance that was at once comical and implacable; he was ready to wrestle the world. His eyes were like black pebbles, tearless and unblinking; that was the Apache of him; but his face was still soft and mobile with boyhood, and his mouth worked against trembling.

Vetch had halted, watching the great good humor of these rough men, knowing there was no malice in their bias. Yet bias it was, reflecting in their voices and words, of which the boy understood enough to spur his savage little soul to retaliation. Vetch sighed. Sara Carver was a fool to let her elder out of her sight—but even as the thought formed he knew it was wrong. She could not shield them forever like a perennial brood hen; sooner or later her copper-skinned pair would have to face the white world on which she had decided for them, sink or swim. Vetch saw no good reason to interfere now.

Reed Toomey was lounging against a gallery post, a thin amusement in his fleshy face, and now he pushed away from the post and sauntered to the edge of the porch, teetering on his heels. He tucked his thumbs in his waistcoat pockets and spoke around his dead cigar. "Why'n't you ask that fellow there, mister? Knows all about this here little breed."

It was the Slovak that Toomey addressed, but his eyes, heavy-lidded with a crafty rancor, settled hard against Vetch. A cold anger touched him; the drummer's deliberate misconstruction had pointed him suddenly toward trouble, the trouble that came of being a man and having pride.

The big Slovak eyed Vetch in a fuddled, slightly drunken way. "Is him you mean?"

"Sure," Toomey murmured. "Ask him."

"Hey, fella. What you know, eh?" The Slovak laughed with a trace of embarrassment, looking furtively at his companions for moral support.

Vetch smiled. "You let it ride. So will I." He took a step toward the boy.

"Hey, fella!" bellowed the Slovak. "Someone pretty light on the wrong side of blanket, I'm think. He maybe yours, the kid, eh?"

Vetch stopped, his weathered face utterly smooth. "Maybe you should soak your head awhile."

"Ho! Is maybe you are making me soak head?"

Vetch shrugged and moved up beside Jimmie Joe, clamping a hand on his shoulder. Instantly the boy's body formed a taut arch of resistance, but Vetch pressed him inexorably forward, past the miners and up the porch steps.

The Slovak's big paw batted Vetch across the

arm. "Hey, you squaw man, I'm ask you—"

Without pausing Vetch finished his stride, then toed around hard and fast and with a wordless savagery drove his fist into the center of the Slovak's red face. The blow budged the big man's jaw by perhaps a fraction of an inch; otherwise he did not even stir, standing huge and rocklike, his long arms loose at his sides. Blood from his pulpy nose cut twin rivulets down the creases at the corners of his thick lips, and he blinked once while the others quietly, warily scattered off from him.

Vetch pushed the boy toward the door, then stepped off the porch and put his back to the wide street, wanting plenty of room. With that concession to his opponent's size, he faced him with a sober patience, just watching.

Very slowly the Slovak lifted one ham of a fist, drawing it across his nose. He studied the blood and lifted his black shaggy brows. "Ho," he said softly. "I'm break you back now—eh!"

He moved on the heel of his grunt, and it was almost a growl, deep-throated and feral. Vetch stepped sideward from his lunge, chopping a bony fist into the Slovak's thick, corded neck above a pulsing vein. It hurt, drawing a vast gulping sigh from the man as he lumbered around.

"Sic 'im, George," drawled a miner, but the others were watchful and silent, as if sensing in the catlike stalk of the Slovak's adversary an enemy who had fought only rarely for fun.

George's small eyes were slitted nearly shut

in his sweating face, and then he smiled almost peacefully. Too late Vetch realized that his half-turning sidestep had put his back to the tie rail, as the Slovak came into him, massive arms sledging powerfully. Vetch felt the wind of two blows he managed to avoid before the small of his back struck the rail. Caught inside the orbit of the Slovak's fist now, he could only duck low and sideways partly to deflect the third swing. Even so, its glancing force rocked his temple. He dropped under a fourth blow, but the Slovak's elbow slammed him brutally across the jaw, half stunning him. He leaned into the big man, trying to clinch for the moment he needed to let his head clear.

The Slovak was slow-moving with drink, but his wits were quick enough; his arms wrapped around the lean scout like prehensile oak trunks, and unhurriedly he applied crushing force. His chest and kettle gut were solid as granite, and with no yield against the constricting power of those arms, Vetch felt his ribs creak and his lungs contract painfully; he fought for air and his chest would not expand. A haze of pain-limned scarlet floated like a frenetic sunburst behind his squinted eyelids. He had not guessed a man could start to lose consciousness so swiftly with his air shut off, and panic threaded the thought; he bent his knees and straightened them, heeling both moccasined feet into George's instep.

The Slovak bellowed, for uncushioned by hard flesh there, he was as vulnerable as any man. Vetch stomped again, now feeling the arms loosen. He drew the hot air deep into his chest and tucked his jaw against his neck, then swung up his head, bringing his skull into a heavy chin. George's teeth clicked together on his tongue, and at the same time Vetch stomped down again.

Howling, the Slovak let him go, and not even bothering to step away, Vetch set himself, his breath sighing through clenched teeth, and smashed his skinned knuckles to the man's bleeding nose. In a sobbing frenzy of bullish fury, the Slovak clouted him backhand, bowling Vetch into the dust. He rolled onto his feet, not caring that his vision was a swimming blur, and wove under the Slovak's arms, slashing at his face before pulling back.

This time he had opened a cut over the miner's eye, and now, forced to scrub at the salty blood that poured into his eye, the big man fought under a handicap. It was easy for Vetch to fall into his own mode of fighting, leaping in and out while he cut his opponent superficially to ribbons, always a step ahead of the Slovak's lagging, mostly one-handed guard and his clumsy slogging blows. The Slovak put Vetch down once more with a blind overhand to the chest, and when Vetch came up he feinted the Slovak to a clear opening and slugged him in the throat. Beyond the haze of exhaustion that misted in his eyes he saw the Slovak's blood-streaked features contort, and knew then that it was over. The big man was hurt, really hurt, though a man might hit him again and again and not put him down.

The Slovak sank on his haunches, holding his throat, a defensive arm lifted palm out. He made a gurgling sound of mighty effort before finding speech. "Is finish—you, fella,—is finish, eh?"

The miners lifted him to his feet. "Come on, George, sleep it off, boy." They propelled his swaying bulk away between them, heading up-street toward a company bunkhouse.

Vetch put his hips against the tie rail and took back his wind. He lifted his hand and licked a bleeding knuckle; the movements brought him to awareness of a score of bruises laced by fiery cuts, of an immense leaden weariness that tugged at every fiber of his body. He had been mauled nearly to insensible numbness, and the real pains and aches would not be felt joint-deep until tomorrow, he knew.

Reed Toomey had been adroit enough to slip away as the fight ended, and now Vetch saw him pass through the batwing doors of the Nugget. A moment later Nick Tana stepped out. He paused, starting to light a cigar, then spotted Vetch, frowned as he snapped his match to the ground, and came on across the street.

Something like an odd ripple of goose flesh along his back caused Vetch abruptly to turn his head. The boy Jimmie Joe stood unmoving by the doorway, and his obsidian eyes bored against Vetch with an intensity totally unre-lieved by any expression. *They never show you a thing*, Vetch thought. *Not a damned thing*. The thought was freighted with an odd discouragement.

Nick reached his side, asking a sharp question as he braced Vetch on his right side, assisting him up the steps. "He roughed up the kid and made some talk," Vetch said. "Forget it, Nick."

"About the kid?" Nick paused before adding shrewdly, "And maybe you too."

"You know the words. Squaw man."

"Sure," Nick said. "Words I heard aplenty when my old man was alive. Got a bitter sound to it even when you know it don't apply, huh?"

"No," Vetch said slowly. "Not that. It was how it was spoke. I don't take that off any man for long. Neither do you."

Nick nodded his understanding, then frowned at the boy and said a single brusque word in Apache. With a startled nod, Jimmie Joe scuttled inside. They followed him into the cool lobby.

Sara Carver was standing by the desk, saying to the clerk in her soft and patient way, "I only want to know if you have seen my—" She broke off speech, a quiet relief in her face as the boy came up beside her. She took his hand with a few scolding words, then fell silent as she saw Vetch come across the lobby with Nick's help. She walked to meet them, and the color lifting under her deep tan indicated her accurate guess at the meaning of his battered face.

She said evenly, "Could this have been on our

account, Mr. Tana? Jimmie Joe's—mine?"

Nick gave a single sober nod. "A bigmouth miner made some talk, ma'am, and pushed your boy around. But you should see him too."

She brought her fingers to her lips, muting her soft, "Oh," and her direct eyes turning on Vetch revealed a shock beyond dismay, as if she had been steeled for anything but this. If she had been prepared for trouble, she had not bargained for the kind that must be met in a man's way; no amount of stiff-lipped woman's pride could stand against the sort of brute abuse that only a strong man could put down.

Without a word then, Sara Carver lent her thin sturdy shoulder to Vetch's weight on his other side. Vetch, embarrassed, was sure that he could make it alone and said so, but they continued to steer him up the stairs and down the hallways to his room. When he had eased into a straight-backed chair, Sara said, "Wait, I'll fetch water."

Vetch shut his eyes and let his head settle loosely on the chair's sharp-edged back. A dull euphoria crept through him. He actually slipped into a half doze, and then the sting of a wet hot cloth on his cuts and bruises brought him harshly alert. Sara's strong hands were gentle; the raw pain ebbed to tolerable aches and he felt drowsy again.

"Mr. Tana."

Sara Carver's quiet voice breaking the silence of the room sluggishly roused him, and he opened his eyes. She was standing by the door where she had paused, the pan of dirty water in her hands. Nick was by the window, staring out, his back to the room, hands in his pockets. He did not look around as she said gently, "Will you tell me something?"

"Ma'am?"

"How is it, being a half-breed?"

Nick did not answer for a full twenty seconds, and when he turned finally and faced them his words came slowly and without rancor. "About like taking what Sam just done, only every day of your life and wondering how to hit back, who your enemy is."

"But do you make such comparisons in your mind? I mean, you have got used to things after a fashion."

"No, ma'am," Nick said calmly. "Not in a lifetime. You live with it and make the best of it, is all. Me, I had the best of such a matter when I think of it. My old man stood up with my squaw mother before a Christian preacher after I was born, so I took what good a breed can from that."

Sara Carver's chin bowed slowly till she stared at the stained water, and her hands grew white-knuckled around the pan rim. A man could only guess at what passed in her mind, but the range of what she had encountered, from a sly drummer through a frightened hotel clerk to a drunken and bellicose miner formed one bitter and irrevocable pattern.

From the next room came the muted wail of the baby.

She shuttled a glance at Vetch, but he knew that nothing could be added to what had been said. She lowered her eyes again and, turning, left the room and closed the door behind her.

Nick rocked on his heels, saying thoughtfully. "A hard way to put it, seeing she has made her choice."

"I don't reckon," Vetch said. "She only thought she had made it. No, you said the right thing, Nick."

Nick gave a somber nod and headed for the door; he said over his shoulder, "Best I leave you and you get some rest."

Vetch conceded this to be a sound notion, and laboriously got to his feet. After pulling the window shade against the harsh midday glare, he stripped down to his underwear. Ruefully he eyed the dirt stains on his suit and the torn shoulder seam of his coat, thinking of his meeting with Miss Vangie. He dropped the coat and trousers with a tired shrug, then crawled into bed and dropped off almost as his head touched the pillow.

Chapter Seven

The gentle click of the latch as someone softly closed the door brought Vetch to a sluggish wakefulness. He rolled to a sitting position in bed and, groaning, rubbed a hand over his face. Early twilight filled the room with dim shadows, but there was enough light to tell that he was alone. Whoever had clicked the latch either had had the wrong room or had entered—and left—for a reason.

Yawning, he swung his feet to the floor and lighted the lamp and, still groggy with sleep, groped for his trousers. He was surprised to find the suit he had tossed carelessly aside draped neatly over the chair back. Wonderingly he shook out coat and trousers and found them carefully cleaned of stains and beaten free of dust; the parted seams of his coat had been mended with small, painstaking stitches. Vetch felt a slow flood of embarrassment, thinking, She *shouldn't have done that*. Somehow the grateful gesture made him feel uneasy and mildly foolish.

She had left his few pocket items, wallet and watch and small change, on the commode; picking up the watch, he found that a good hour remained before he had to pick up Miss Vangie Armitage at her shop. His body ached from a multitude of bruises, and he almost dreaded to inspect his face in the shaving mirror; he was relieved to discover no mark but a faint swelling along his jaw.

After dressing he reached for his worn shell belt and holstered gun as naturally as he would his hat. He would feel downright naked, going out on a street unarmed. But a gun was a tool of the violence that Miss Vangie deplored, and in her neat small parlor it always felt heavy and conspicious even under his coat. With what was riding on this evening's courtship, he had best take no chances. When he left his room the gun remained.

He was mildly relieved not to find Sara Carver among those in the hotel dining room. Women had always made him awkward, but never Sara Carver until now—

He ordered and ate a thick steak, fried potatoes, and apple pie, washing it all down with strong black coffee: modest fare that he could never get enough of after long patrols on bacon and hardtack. Perhaps his taste would become more finicky with settled life and home cooking; his thoughts drifting to Miss Vangie Armitage became fretted by sudden doubts. Her answer would decide in a very real sense the whole course of his life.

He found himself on the hotel porch, savoring the cool dusk and the smoke of his after-supper cigar, watching the glow of Miss Vangie's shop window on the well-lighted upper street. The whole town was bustling on this pay-day night, and the shops and bars would be open till late. Vetch ground his cigar under a heel and consulted his watch. Fifteen minutes yet. His palm sweated around the metal case. He had time for a drink, and he needed one.

He quartered across the well-trafficked street and passed through the Nugget's smoky, jostling din to the bar where Nick Tana was still drinking in cheerful defiance of the traditional Indian vulnerability to liquor. Vetch ordered his drink as Nick gave him a dry study, saying, "Leastways he didn't track up your face."

"About the only place he didn't." Vetch set his elbows on the bar and scowled at his image in the back-bar mirror.

Nick remarked mildly, "She fix up your coat?"

"Yeah." Vetch felt slightly ruffled. "How about a drink?"

"You know better'n to give an Injun firewater," Nick said soberly. "However, seeing's I have had several."

"Ho-ho!" A massive hand descended between Vetch's shoulders as he swallowed his whisky.

Then George the Slovak made solicitous noises, hammering the coughing Vetch gently on the back until his definite sensation of strangling on liquid fire ebbed. "Is too bad. She's go down the wrong way, eh? I am have the fun with you, squaw man, that's all."

"Glad you weren't mad," Vetch told him dourly; the hamlike palm falling on his shoulder almost drove him to his knees.

"Ho-ho!" the Slovak roared. "You good fella. Now I'm buy you new drink. I'm plenty like man who fight like you. Eh!"

Somebody said softly, "Your night's over, Georgie. Anyhow you had a skinful." The man who spoke was rawboned and slab-muscled. He wore the rough clothes of a miner, but his derby hat and a heavy coiled bullwhip looped over his shoulder gave him a look of crude authority. Vetch knew him. Shug Mayhaw, foreman of the Merry Widow mine. He had a hard grin and the reputation of a driver and a bully boy.

Mayhaw raised his voice, glancing over the room. "Listen, all you Merry Widow buckos. You mind we're runnin' four six-hour shifts a day to meet a lease deadline. Ones o'you who are on next shift should be soaking your heads. I got a wagon outside and I want to see you all piled on inside o'five minutes."

The Slovak blinked foggily, the big, vapid smile fading from his battered face. "Not me," he announced. "I'm no going—"

Shug Mayhaw's lean arm twitched, flipping up the long-barreled Colt rammed in his belt.

He laid the muzzle across George's skull with a cool, practiced tap. The Slovak plunged face down in the sawdust.

"Pretty rough," Vetch observed.

Shug Mayhaw laughed silently. He was fairly drunk himself, with a controlled and wicked drunkenness. "Yeah, Injun tracker. And could get rougher."

Vetch shrugged and swung back to the bar. It was no business of his. Mayhaw stalked about the room, roaring orders and curses, yanking miners out of their chairs and shoving them toward the door. They were a reluctant and sullen crew as they filed out. Mayhaw ordered a couple of men to carry out the Slovak, and he followed them.

Vetch ordered another drink and took it quickly. "That's all, Nick. Time to see a lady."

Nick looked compassionate and remotely maudlin. He saluted with his glass. "G'luck attend you, chief."

Vetch went out the batwing doors and paused to straighten his coat. Shug Mayhaw had his evening shift well in hand; they were clustered around a water trough, ducking themselves or scooping water over their heads. Mayhaw, grinning, grabbed one fuddled miner by the neck and held his head under the water till he began to splash and kick. A high-sided ore wagon with a horse hitch was pulled up by the sidewalk, and the somewhat sobered men began climbing in.

Vetch headed for the upper street at a saunter, his belly full of moths. He kept nervously fumbling with his lapels and tie, unable to convince himself that they were neat. Nearing the millinery shop, he saw the abundant figure of Mrs. Thatcher step out against the light, a package under her arm. That meant Miss Vangie was closing for the day, and he quickened his pace.

Suddenly a rattle of harness and a savage whip crack drew his glance backward. The ore wagon had lunged forward as Shug Mayhaw on the seat plied his bullwhip around the horses' heads. The animals were straining the wagon into motion, and it swiftly gained momentum.

Vetch came to a stop. The drunken fool—and on a street full of women and kids. People were already scrambling out of the wagon's path, but just ahead Vetch saw a light ranch rig swing from a cross street in perfect time for a collision with Mayhaw's team. A small, frightened girl was standing in the center of the street, wailing her head off. In perhaps two seconds Vetch catalogued these and other crosscurrents of the busy avenue that added to disaster unless that wagon were halted.

He was already in movement as the heavy vehicle rumbled abreast of him. Reaching the right lead animal, Vetch caught the headstall and ran with the team, swinging his weight into a stubborn effort to brake down their rampaging run before it was beyond control. He heard Mrs. Thatcher's piercing shriek and Mayhaw's bullroaring curse. The team began dragging to a shuffling, heaving stop.

The Stalking Moon

Vetch spoke quietly to the animals as the wildness left them. Then came the pistol-shot crack of the whip; pain ribboned flatly across Vetch's shoulder and arm. Letting go the head-stall, he came around on his heel as Mayhaw's whip arm pulled back again.

Vetch took two quick steps that carried him inside the orbit of the foreman's next vicious swing. He was nearly to the wagon when the lash came down, and he hunched his head and threw up an arm. The weak force of the upper whip fell on his spread palm, and Vetch made a fist and yanked savagely. Mayhaw, on his feet to put his shoulder fully behind the blows, came close to falling over the side. He saved himself by releasing the whip handle, only to grab at the Colt in his belt. Hastily thumbing back the hammer, he brought up the weapon and fired.

Vetch, still awkwardly holding the whip, heard a jangling cascade of breaking glass somewhere behind him as the wild shot found a window. Now he dropped the whip and with the same hand swept back his coat skirt. Mayhaw was already recocking the gun, this time swinging it squarely to bear. His eyes were maniacal. Vetch's hand brushed his weaponless hip; then he remembered and could only stand flat-footed and helpless. There was no time even to brace for the bullet.

The shot came, but not from Mayhaw's gun. He was sagging down against the seat, clutching a bloody arm. Vetch turned his eyes till he located Nick Tana standing not a dozen paces to his right. A pale trickle of smoke wisped from his leveled pistol.

Vetch drew and let out a sighing breath. "Fair piece of shooting for a lickered Apache."

"Hell it was," Nick said. "I meant to kill the white son of a—" He paused to look about him, noticed a pair of ladies on the sidewalk and politely tipped his hat to them. "—the loco son of a gun."

The fat and officious town marshal huffed up and aimlessly demanded explanations. Vetch stated his part with brevity and said he did not want to press charges. He was tolerant of brutality because he knew at first hand the things that turned men like Mayhaw into brutes and he felt no condemnation. Sam Vetch had been through it all.

Nick ambled back to the Nugget, the marshal herded Shug Mayhaw away to the doctor, and the crowd began to break up. Some late arrivals pestered Vetch with questions, but he put them off curtly. He headed on for Miss Vangie's shop, noting the great gaping hole in the window of the adjacent mercantile store where Mayhaw's shot had gone. That racket must have scared the devil out of her, Vetch thought, and quickened to a run as he palmed open the door of her shop.

She was facing a counter, leaning both hands against it. Her face was waxen and pinched in the saffron glow of an overhead lamp. Her eyes held the wild strain of shock, and she seemed to look through him.

Vetch took a few steps and halted. "Miss Vangie."

She blinked; her throat muscles quivered. "Sam, I was standing outside by the window when the bullet—the bullet only missed me."

Vetch felt cold-sick himself, but he put only a gentle urgency in his voice. "It is all over now." He took another step and he wanted with a sudden hunger to touch her, to lend her what comfort his strength could give. Self-consciously he let his half-raised hand fall to his side and said again, lamely, "It is all over."

"What?" She turned a dazed look on him. "What did you say?" She shut her eyes and rubbed a hand over her pale cheek. "Oh—oh, I'm sorry. You said—yes. I saw it, Sam. You didn't have your gun, did you? Why, you—you could have been killed. Did you leave it behind because of—"

"That don't matter, ma'am. It is finished now, and no great harm done."

"No harm?" She repeated the words like a mechanical toy running down. "No harm done? But it was all the harm in the world. Don't you see?"

For a moment he eyed her with an uneasy perplexity, and then put out his hand. "Miss Vangie."

She shrank against the counter, her gaze fixed on his hand. "Please don't touch me," she said in a calm and matter-of-fact voice. "I am afraid that I may scream if you do."

The words were like a knife, the knife that

cuts deep and silent and kills quickly. He simply stood and watched her face, which was full of the bright hard calm that masks hysteria. Then the mask crumpled. Her hand came up to her mouth; her eyes darkened to an appalled realization. She turned swiftly away from him, clasping both hands to her cheeks. A trapped little sound left her.

Vetch did not move, waiting, not knowing what to say and miserable because there had to be some way of words that would make all things sound again. Something in him blindly refused to accept what had just passed. She turned around finally, her small face reflecting the composure of bitter acceptance. Seeing it, Vetch felt a last nameless hope curl up in him and die stillborn.

She said gently, "Oh, Sam. It would never have worked. What is there to say other than I'm sorry? Unless it's that a little hurt now is better than—No, that is all wrong, isn't it? There is no little hurt." A reserve of courage stiffened her back; her eyes were very clear. "Truth is better than consolation, Sam. Put me in the finest of houses and I would still never feel safe unless I knew there were other houses on each side, and streets and lights and people. Perhaps I will never have to call for a policeman, but I need to know that there is one within the sound of my voice. So I am going back to all of that, but alone."

Vetch had closed his jaws so tightly they were aching, he realized. "I want to understand this."

"No," she said, and quick tears sparkled in her eyes. "That's the whole of it, don't you see?—you can never understand me any more than I could grasp why you would die if taken away from this wild country. What need has a man like you of any policemen—or even laws? The way you rose to the occasion out there—so magnificently—why, you make your own laws and enforce them too. Something I'd never realized before is how perfectly you are one with the people and country, the whole life here. I had persuaded myself that what separated us was a matter of—of upbringing or training. But it's so much more. We were born—yes, born—very different people, you and I."

She swallowed with the stress of feeling; her voice cracked and faltered. "Each of us—each of us alive is in the final sense an island, Sam. Until we die we live with the pain of knowing that. Pain that we can make tolerable and push into the background only by knowing and sharing with another. We need that much so badly that sometimes we go too far to find it."

Her lips were trembling uncontrollably as she came to him; the crisp rustle of her dress and the scent of heliotrope and her warm closeness enveloped his awareness. And she stepped back. Miserably he wanted to speak, but she turned away from him. There was nothing more to be said.

Chapter Eight

He lay in the darkness of his sweltering room and smoked three thick cigars to inch-long stubs, occasionally stretching his arm to tap off ashes on the marble-topped washstand. Otherwise he did not stir a muscle. Sprawled bonelessly on the lumpy mattress in all his clothes, his dirty boots crossed carelessly on the rumpled blanket, he stared fixedly at the black ceiling and wondered all over again about things. For the hundredth time everything raveled away into a blank indifference; what did it matter now?

After leaving Miss Vangie's shop he had gone perhaps a half block when the delayed reaction had hit him fully, washing through him with a pain that was physical and leaving him with a terrifying emptiness that was like nothing he had ever known. All that he had planned and built had gone for nothing, a blow all the more paralyzing for being unexpected. He had centered every hope for his future around one woman; never a vain man, he had yet felt a deep, stubborn certainty that had refused to admit the possibility of a turndown.

He had turned briefly into the nearest saloon and had set out to get drunk, but for all the effect he might have downed as many shots of water, and he soon quit.

In the dark room now, Vetch smoked on in a bleak musing till a nauseous ache in his temples made a dull intrusion on apathy; coughing, he stabbed out the last cigar and swung to his feet, as loggy as a drugged man. He had not bothered to open the window; when he lighted the lamp now, the acrid smoke made a heavy blue mist. He stumbled to the window and barked his knees on the sill, and, swearing wearily, muscled up the warped sash. A hot wind stirred through the room, along with a flood of boisterous sound from the lower street, where the fever of boom-town excitement grew with the deepening night.

He lighted the lamp on the commode, filled the wash basin, and splashed tepid wetness over his head. As he dried himself on a ragged towel, someone tapped on the door. He opened it to find Sara Carver there, holding her baby, who was wakeful and restless; she rocked him gently.

"Mr. Vetch." Though she appeared calm, her

voice shook perceptibly; she frowned at this and lowered her gaze to the baby as she continued. "I have had to think about what happened today. This is not easy to say. Oh, I suppose I shouldn't bother you at such an hour. Tomorrow—"

"Better step inside and tell it."

She hesitated, and then, stiff and still-faced, moved past him into the room. Vetch left the door a little ajar and motioned her to the single chair. She was unmoving; the lamplight was not kind to her weather-darkened face. Her lips remained tightly compressed, and after a moment he said with a bare patience, "Yes'm?"

"I don't know how to say it. All the trouble we have put you to already, and for nothing."

"Nothing?"

"Yes. I have changed my mind. Or the things I've seen have changed it. I think that I could face anything on my account alone, but I can't—I have no right—to make that decision for the children, not when they have all their lives before them." There was no stain of feeling in her face or the Indian flatness of her words. Yet her inward-turned gaze seemed to see past all surfaces to what they had not seen. "Why should a child be made to suffer, Mr. Vetch, unless being born is a sin? Here—my children are half-breed bastards. No. There'll be bitterness enough—no matter what's done—without saddling them with that and making good people like the Jerrolds share our trouble."

Vetch said slowly, "I ain't sure I follow you,

ma'am. What else can you do?"

"I thought that I had told you. At the first way station."

Vetch was a few seconds in grasping her meaning. "You'll go back to the Apaches to stay?" He waited for her nod, then wheeled toward the window; he scowled down at the checkering of lamplight on the dust of the street. "Army and the Indian agency might have things to say concerning that."

"I will take that chance. If you will do me a last kindness and lend me stage fare back to Fort Sutro. Then I sha'n't bother you again."

For the space of a full minute Vetch stared at the street, letting the idea form, knowing it was born of a kind of desperation and for that reason should almost certainly be quietly discarded. Yet his mind picked only half-heartedly at the token objection—*A couple of desperate people, and nothing good can come out of that*—and then reached sudden decision and let it quickly harden.

He turned from the window and came across the room, halting near her to look at the baby. Its arm gently flailed the air; Vetch grinned and tickled the brown palm and let the tiny hand close around his finger. "It strikes me I ain't caught this fellow's name."

"Carl—after my father."

The little fingers seemed dry and feeble in their hold, and again Vetch was touched by a disturbing impression; infants of this age had hefty grips and could often support their own weights. He raised his eyes to Sara Carver's face, and her expression told him nothing.

"I am going on to New Mexico," he told her. "You want to come along and bring them— well, maybe we can work things out."

Faint lines of puzzlement formed around her eyes. "I'm afraid that I don't—"

"My ranch in New Mexico." He ducked his head and uneasily scrubbed a palm over his jaw. "Maybe you would want to go with me there."

For ten full seconds she did not answer, and then: "You're not joking—no, I can see that you're not. A quite generous suggestion, Mr. Vetch." Her words came thin and brittle. "One that I can hardly believe your bride will appreciate."

Vetch made no effort to keep the harshness from his voice as he told of the change forced on his plans. When he had finished she nodded and said, "I see," but her eyes were strange, as though comprehension still eluded her. And she said, "You would not—you can't be proposing marriage to me."

"Why not?" he said brusquely. "I can offer you a home, a damn good home. I built that place for—for a lifetime. A place where your kids can grow and not be hurt by clacking tongues. It is that far a piece from town and neighbors. Well—best if you think on it awhile."

He knew that the bitterness roiling in him roughened his words, and he hardly cared; he wanted only to salvage what he could of his broken plans. Sara Carver's face was utterly still in the half shadow; slowly she stepped past him to the window to stare out. "I didn't say the half of it before—generosity indeed." Her brief, taut laugh came, like an icicle snapping. "Except that I don't need your pity or your home or—"

"Pity," he broke in with honest wonderment. "Is that what you think?"

"What else can I?"

Vetch ran a hand through his hair, a gesture that summed up all the frayed tiredness a man could feel. "I don't know, ma'am. It ain't rightly important to you what I had in mind, I reckon. It is just we might do each other some good this way. That is taking a long chance maybe, but I don't see that you got any choice. To be honest, whether you believe it or don't, neither do I."

It was hard to go on, but he said the words somehow, telling of a man's need to fill the home he had made with more than empty dreams. There was nothing offensive or startling to his proposal as far as convention went; a woman with a half-dozen children might be widowed one day and wedded again by the next, for the fierce exigencies of the frontier left no option. When and where need arose, it was met by swift and practical improvisation; this could be the only rule where rules did not exist.

That much Sara Carver could accept, but her tempered pride demanded a reciprocal bargain where she might give as well as take. Vetch understood this without being told, and he watched her face. Her eyes began to change; her expression relented without thawing, and he knew what the answer would be.

"I'll marry you if you like," she said in a flat, almost indifferent tone. "Of course you're not insensible to what you are taking on in the way of civilized penalties. No matter how far you are from people, they talk."

"Hens cackle too." Vetch scowled. "I ain't given a tinker's damn what people thought for so long, reckon I just don't mind looking like a damned fool."

Her eyes kindled with a brief warmth. "You're a good man, Sam Vetch, much too good for what you are taking on yourself. Believe me, I am grateful. I'll do the very best by my part of the bargain that the circumstances allow."

"No need to wait then," Vetch said. "The local J.P. can do the job right away, tonight. We'll take the first stage out." He paused a bleak moment. "The place is finished and furnished, and Hilario and Ned—they're my hands—will have things in good running order. We can be there in a few days and move in directly."

"Whatever you say." Sara started for the door, and there halted uncertainly. "May I bring Jimmie Joe? He is sleeping, but I shouldn't want him to wake and find me gone." She shook her head. "No, that's not really it. I want him with us; he must understand what is happening. But if you would rather—"

"Can't see a reason why not."

Minutes later, when Sara and Jimmie Joe joined him in the hallway, he had wry cause to regret his ready agreement. The boy's face was scrubbed to a glow; his black hair was slick and neat as a seal's pelt, and it was plain from his look of raging but bridled hostility that he understood only too well. His mother was taking a hated *pinda-likoyee*, a white-eyes, as husband; and the thin toleration he had allowed Vetch had evaporated in a child's pure hatred. *Now I'm the enemy*, Vetch thought grimly. *Well then, he will have to grow out of it is all*.

They went down the stairs and past the desk accompanied by the brittle stares of the desk clerk and the usual sprinkling of lobby loafers. *The word has gone forth*, Vetch thought. A breed was bottom man on the social scale in this border country; the woman who bore breed children and the man who befriended her could count on being lumped in.

They reached the street and turned north, Vetch shouldering a path for the woman and boy through the thin surges of drunken, brawling miners. Roughly breasting the swirl of white people for them gave a first wry substance to his future, as a buffer between his new family and the world. *There's a happy thought for a man's wedding night*.

Coming into the darkened upper town, they left the crowded walks and booming revelry behind; Vetch took Sara Carver's elbow and she moved silently beside him, her eyes fixed straight ahead. A cold and unaccountable restraint seemed to have settled between them like a tangible force. To Vetch it framed a baffling irritation, for their relation till now had been as good as events would allow. He could even concede Nick's observation that Sara Carver had for a time looked up to him. Allowing for the impersonality of the bargain they had now established, she might show a spark or two of the warmth he had seen in her from time to time. She did not, and oddly this troubled him. He hadn't a notion of what was wrong, and he could not put a bald query to her.

They were a block from the justice's home when he felt obliged to break silence. "Should of mentioned the coat. You done a fine job of sewing on it."

"Thank you. Let's stop here," she murmured, and they halted in the sketchy blackness of shadows flung by the row of skimpy cottonwoods lining this residential block. He could see her eyes plainly; they were now fixed on his face and were strangely luminous. "I can't let you go into this without knowing the truth, all of the truth. I told you that you killed the man who was my husband. That was not true."

Vetch gave a weary nod, and her eyes widened faintly. "Then you knew?"

"A guess. Not mine, Nick Tana's."

She said without emotion, "My husband was Salvaje. Did Nick Tana tell you that? Do you know who Salvaje is?"

Again he nodded, and after a moment he heard her deep indrawing sigh. "Well, there's little else to tell. After I was captured by Toriano I was taken into Mexico—that you know. I first saw Salvaje in their camp in the Sierra Madre; he came out of nowhere one night to Susto's *jacal*. Susto was the Indian who captured me. He was Salvaje's brother, the man you and the sergeant shot. The woman you wounded, his wife Neeta, became my sister-in-law. It was not a usual thing for them to take white women prisoners, but even as a slave I was only worked hard, never harmed. No man wanted me—I was too strange for them—until Salvaje saw me. He did not ask; he demanded and received. Nobody, even Toriano, would dare raise an objection if he had one. They called Salvaje Ya-ik-tee, and thought he was not human. Sometimes— sometimes I almost agreed with them."

A breeze disturbed the high branches; the shadow across her face broke and showed the frown gathering her straight brows. "He was different from the others; I think he would have been even if his life had not warped by—But that is a long story. Being aware that he was strange, and of the effect it had, he mocked them by working at his eccentricities. He had never taken a wife since he could have taken as many as he wished, but to take a white slave as wife—ah, that was different."

Vetch raised a blunt question that had haplessly occupied him for some time. "How did he use you?"

"Well enough, I suppose." The question seemed not to have occurred to her before. "Not gently, not brutally. Almost with indifference. In the first place I saw him infrequently; his forays away from the tribe lasted weeks, months, and he might rejoin for a day and a night, rarely longer. Further, I was never an individual to him—just a faceless specimen of another race. My being a woman was simply incidental to his real reason for wedding me. He did beat me once. And to be honest, I deserved it." The corners of her mouth lifted slightly. "As to my feelings otherwise—I was afraid of him, not because of anything he ever said or did. It was just his way. The only ones never afraid of him were Susto and Jimmie Joe—his brother and his son. With this baby, they made his only living ties. And there was Neeta; she took to beating me and threatening my life for the reason I told you. Jealousy."

"But it was her husband's brother you married."

"She wanted her husband's brother," Sara said matter-of-factly. "She had always wanted Salvaje, and he could not have cared less; she told me so every time she beat me, though never when Susto was about. If Susto had known her feeling he would have cut off her nose."

Vetch scraped a heel against the earth, scowling downward. "That clears up things some. Except I would like to know why you didn't see fit to say this before."

"I'm not sure now," she said tiredly. "When that man at the way station, Henery, was telling about the murdered rancher and his family I knew at once whose work it was and why he had come north, to get news of his brother and his two children. Killing Mexicans is, I think, as near to a religion as he ever had; it would take this strong a reason to lure him out of Mexico. I suppose that my simple blind impulse was to throw Salvaje off my trail, or to convince myself that I was doing so, by cutting clean any remote possibility of my name's being coupled with his. That is why, minutes later, I told you a near-complete fabrication. I—I know it was foolish."

After a moment Vetch said quietly, "You are riding a notion he'll try to track you down? Never heard of anything like that."

"Listen to me." Her hand went out to his arm, her fingers making an unconscious pressure. "Don't, as you value your life, judge him by any men you have ever known, Indian or white. Nor try to predicate his next move on any basis of logic. He never followed rules, but made his own, though I believe that pure whim governed most of his actions. And he will make you play his game in his way."

"You seem almighty sure about this, about him looking for you," Vetch said skeptically.

"No, not me. The children. I have the children, you see."

Her quiet certainty was impressive enough so that Vetch did not feel inclined to deprecate it. But he said, "He won't be following you to New Mexico, anyway."

"I have the children," she repeated; the night wind rising off the distant flats was warm and yet she shivered, then gave a soft, strained laugh. "New Mexico, of course. How could he find us even here, much less in New Mexico?" Her gaze came to steady focus, meeting his. "And this does not change anything?"

"I call it a good start," he said gruffly, and held out his hands. "I'll take the young'un now."

A perceptible quiver ran through Sara Carver; but then, very slowly, she laid the sleeping infant in his arms. Again they moved back into step toward Justice Todson's house, the boy reluctantly dragging his steps behind them. As they walked, Vetch felt the woman's light and timorous touch on his wrist, and then her hand slipped into the bend of his arm and stayed there.

Chapter Nine

The town of Spanish Crossing made a minor if unsightly scar on the green foothill country that bordered the Soledad River Basin toward the east. Situated on the river tributary of Spanish Creek, the town was connected to the railhead city of Soledad fifty miles to the south only by a mud-rutted road that had briefly sustained a twice-a-week stage run on which some backwoods entrepreneur had lost his hickory shirt. All that remained of his defunct enterprise was a battered mud wagon now belonging to the Soledad Livery barn.

Mindful that they would still face a long horseback ride after reaching Spanish Crossing, Sam Vetch, when he left the train at Soledad, went directly to the livery barn and haggled the proprietor into letting him rent his mud wagon. Little haggling was required, since the proprietor was getting a bargain at any price, in renting an idle vehicle and saving the cost of a driver by sending his son along to drive the mud wagon back to Soledad.

So Vetch transported his new family to Spanish Crossing in comparative comfort, Sara and the two boys riding in the coach while he rode topside with the garrulous young driver, paying no need whatever to his simpleminded ramblings.

Vetch had not a twinge of regret concerning the strange marriage and proxy fatherhood to which he had committed himself; he had not exaggerated in telling Sara that his own circumstances were as quietly desperate as hers. He found nothing noble in the knowledge that he had simply salvaged the best that he could from his ruined plans.

Given time and patience, he judged that he and Sara could arrive at a common ground that would be adequate for a life together. Her stark and lonely courage had been above question from the first, and he had seen her merciless honesty when the chips were down. Her native intelligence, broadened by an extent of education rare among women of the times, might have meant a life of harsh frustration as a ranch wife in remote mountain country. Instead, because a strong and disciplined mind had been her salvation in those years of captivity that had superbly tempered her native qualities, being a fit mate for a rough-living rancher should prove a relatively slight hardship to her.

A far larger doubt would overshadow the absorption of the two children into the pattern of his life, and it was clear that the boy Jimmie Joe, already shaped in another direction, would be his big headache. This much of the shape of things to come was well settled in his mind by the time they rolled into the crooked muddy lane that formed Spanish Crossing's single street.

Vetch hauled up the team by a saloon porch where they could step down without going ankle-deep in mud. He paid the boy and passed him the reins, then got down and opened the coach door and swung Sara and the baby to the porch. Jimmie Joe made a little spring from the wagon to the dry boards. As they started down the street toward the local livery stable Sara fell behind Vetch, and half absently he slowed up to accommodate her stride. When she still lagged behind him, he had a quick realization that made him say quietly, "Walk up beside me."

She started, and a little color lifted to her face. "I—I'm sorry. I wasn't thinking." She moved to his side and he took her arm, and they walked on. Vetch squelched the unwonted irritation he felt, knowing that it was in such small surface matters that he would need patience. She could not shed overnight the unwitting habits of an Indian woman, such as staying meekly to the rear of her husband.

Shortly Vetch was dickering with the stableman, a crusty middle-aged widower named Dodd, for the rent of three horses. He kept hedging on the price, and presently Vetch said, "Tom, if there's something else on your mind, get it out."

Dodd shuttled a cold and pointed glance at the brown-faced baby in Sara's arms. "I heard you were courting over in Arizona, but I was give to understand she was a maiden lady."

"Maybe you heard wrong. Happen that is all, you want to talk business now?"

"I ever tell you my brother was killed by Injuns?"

"No. You want to talk business?"

"Sam, there's plenty people around here who lost kin and friends when the siwashes was rampaging not so many years ago. They ain't going to take kindly to this."

"That's too bad." A wicked rashness was hardening in Vetch; he knew that it was purely defensive and foolish, that this was no way to win over wrongheads; but he had worn his own rut through life too long, with apology to no man, to like being crowded on a business that was his own and nobody else's.

Dodd scowled. "I'll rent you horses, seeing it's twenty miles to your place. You have Ned or the Mex bring them in. After that, I won't be wantin' trade with Injun mixers. I don't want no fight with you on this, Sam. I am just saying how it's got to be."

After a moment Vetch said quietly, "All right, Tom, that's fair. So long as you let it lay at that.

If it comes back to me that you have made any loose talk after today, I'll come to call you out. Anyone else, too. I mean that."

"I know you do," Dodd said gruffly, and looked at his son, who was leaning in the stable archway, resting an arrogant stare on Jimmie Joe. "Matt, saddle up three, one sidesaddle. Hop to it, hear?"

"Sure, Pa." The Dodd boy pushed away from the archway. He was about eleven and large for his age. As he moved into the runway his idle sidestep carried him full into Jimmie Joe, and the point of his shoulder knocked the smaller boy sprawling. Jimmie Joe rolled silently to his feet and lunged without preliminary at the stableman's son.

Vetch was already in motion, and now he grabbed Jimmie Joe's thin shoulders and held him as he kicked and writhed. A word from his mother made him subside, his eyes like black stones again.

"I tripped, Pa," Matt said, not quite grinning.

Dodd said harshly, "Do as I told you," and the boy slouched down the runway. Dodd wheeled into his office and did not come out until the horses were readied. He tersely named a sum; Vetch paid him without a word, mounted Sara on the sidesaddled animal, lifted Jimmie Joe into saddle and shortened his stirrups, then stepped into his own saddle. The boy Matt, again leaning in the archway, spat at the ground as they rode out past him.

The hour was early, and Vetch set an easy

pace along the ill-defined trail made by the rare comings and goings of him and his two hands. Over the time that he had intermittently spent developing his outfit he had mentally charted a likely route from Spanish Crossing to his ranch with an eye to the day when a wagon road would negotiate those rocky grades and mottes of dense timber, switch-backing across this massive ridge or blasted through where that flinty spur rose. The day was still distant, but he resignedly knew that civilization finally would eat into his lonely backwoods; however he disliked the whole business, he had to prepare against its coming. So that it was only in a half-joking vein that he said to Sara now, "We are such a whoop and a holler from much of anywhere, we'll have to build a school for the kids."

"If we can obtain a few books and writing materials," she said seriously, "I am well qualified to teach them."

Vetch nodded, wishing that she were less somber, but again he was reckoning with the Indian influence. Shut off by race and culture from the tribe's lighter pastimes, she had assumed their way of masking her vital feelings in any alien situation.

Yet she seemed to enjoy the ride, remarking on the vistas of pine-flanked slopes and vast meadows of sun-cured grass that made this northern high country an unblemished paradise. Vetch continued at a slow pace, often calling halts to rest the horses, and Sara seemed more lighthearted with each relaxed mile that they placed between them and whatever civilization Spanish Crossing might represent.

First darkness had marched in black and indigo patterns across the land and sky when they came off a wooded bench onto a long, plunging slope that dipped into a broad vale enclosed on this and the two flanking sides by rounded, semi-timbered hills and on the far side by a great ridge of weathered granite; beyond the hills to left and right sprawled the long, well-grassed valleys that made this prize range. Down in the vale moonlight bathed in strong relief the low rambling log house and its log outbuildings, snugly framed by the tall hills and the ridge. The windows of the long bunkhouse-cook shack set off below the house were warm with lamplight, and Vetch was warmed by the sense of a real homecoming. This was not altogether as he had planned it, but at long last he was coming back to stay.

He took Sara directly to the house, knowing that, womanlike, the interior of her new home would command her first attention. And her pleasure, from the moment he let them inside and lighted a lamp, was all he could have hoped for from the woman he had brought to the place he had painstakingly furnished for another woman.

The furniture was heavy oak, gleaming and new; he had put in a full week of trips to Spanish Crossing in conveying the furnishings here on a two-horse drag. Making a pleasant contrast to its weighty dark formality were the rough log walls hung with a colorful heterogeneity of hunting trophies and rare weapons and the bright barbarism of Navajo blankets.

Vetch led the horses to the corral and turned them in, helped by his two hands, Coombs and Cortinas, who had tramped from the bunkhouse to greet him. Afterward he took them to the house and introduced them to his new family.

Ned Coombs was a shriveled, white-haired bit of a man with a wry brown face deeply furrowed by age and weather and continually screwed into a surly pucker, as if he had bitten into something sour.

Hilario Cortinas was a slender, wiry, taciturn Mexican in his indefinite thirties; his eyes of a glassy pale blue in his coffee-brown face showed his Anglo background. He spoke so softly that a man automatically cocked an ear when he began to talk, which was rarely. He dragged a stiff and useless right leg.

It was that crippled leg on Cortina's part, and on Coombs's his advanced years, that had brought them to Vetch's payroll. He had stretched to a limit in building and stocking his outfit and he could pay neither man more than a pittance for holding down the place during his absences. This was satisfactory to them, for though both were capable of a hard day's work at any range job, no employing ranchers they knew would allow them even a chance. Vetch had not hesitated to hire them on a trial basis, nor, after both men had proven themselves, to assure them of a good wage when he could afford it. These were hard men to know, taciturn and withdrawn and solitary and fully content with their lot on a remote ranch, though only a common temperament permitted their toleration of one another. Old Ned's hidebound hatred of "pope lovers" and "greasers," like the whole incredible range of his crotchety prejudices, was vehement and unreasoning. Yet they worked well in harness, and Vetch worked well with either or both; since most of the old man's bias was pure bark, he could grin it away.

Or had until now. Ned's hackles began to bristle as soon as he laid eyes on Sara's sons, and he promptly left for the bunkhouse after refusing her offer for coffee. Hilario drank two cups of the strong fresh brew and gave polite thanks before taking his leave.

"Not very good coffee, was it?" Sara said quietly.

"Good and strong," Vetch smiled. "Give yourself time. And old Coombs too."

"Yes, time," she mused, not meeting his eyes. "We need a lot of that, don't we? I'll put the children to bed."

Vetch sat in the parlor and thumbed through a stockman's journal while she established Jimmie Joe in one of the bedrooms. The baby would sleep in their room. For now, until Vetch could fashion something better, his crib would be a box on a table.

Presently she came to the doorway and said

tonelessly, "Will you come to bed now?"

Vetch, suddenly occupied with lighting a cigar, puffed hearty clouds of smoke. "Oh—ah, go ahead. I'll be along." His hands were shaking as he waved out the match; he told himself that he was only being considerate of her natural reticence under the circumstances. The fact was that he was as downright scared as he could ever remember feeling. It was a full fifteen minutes before he nervously stabbed out the cigar butt and extinguished the lamp.

The bedroom was dark as he entered; he could hear the baby breathing softly in sleep, but there was no sound from the master bed. In a few minutes he slid gingerly between the covers and lay tensely awake, staring into the darkness. She had made not a move or sound, yet he could feel the depression her weight made and the subtle aura of her warmth under the blankets. He knew that she was not asleep, and yet he did not know what would be right to do or say. Gripped by perplexity, he did nothing for some minutes, and then thinking, *The hell with it—don't think*, stirred onto his side and touched her with his hand.

Still she said nothing, but she was as passive as clay; an increasing conviction that something was wrong made him about to withdraw his hand when she spoke almost inaudibly. "I'm sorry, but please. Not yet. I'm sorry."

He lay on his back, wide awake and unmoving, remembering her words, *We need a lot of time*, and now came his silent answer, swarming with every doubt that he had put aside: *But how much—how long?*

The baby began to cry, soft, choking cries broken by little muffled coughs.

Chapter Ten

The days of his new life, each one strange and distinctive at first, fell into a gradual pattern and seemed to run together, pleasantly and not-so-pleasantly. It was good to come home after a hard day to a woman in a clean dress who kept a neat house and who willingly learned to prepare the things he liked. He did not blame her for her continuing incapacity to love as a woman; she had been used too long to satisfy a man's insensate if not brutal demands, and for that alone. He knew that she would submit if he demanded, but he did not want her that way; he preferred to hope that time would heal and bring change, but things got no better.

The same was true of all his gestures toward the boy Jimmie Joe. Vetch dredged up a hundred memories of his own boyhood, of things he and his father had done together, things he and other boys had enjoyed doing most. Some of them seemed a bit silly at this distance, and he wondered whether such pastimes might not seem trivial and incomprehensible to an Indian boy.

Then he thought of those pleasures that crossed cultural and age differences between men and boys everywhere. He found time, time that he could not easily spare from his work, to take Jimmie Joe on hunting and fishing forays. It was perfect country for these diversions, with its miles of virgin forest and many high, cold lakes and streams. If anything could break down the boy's reserve, it should be the roar of a hunter's gun or the strike of a flashing trout. Yet the boy was able, hour after hour through week on week, to keep a mechanical composure, never extending himself an iota past the bare toleration he had shown almost from the beginning.

Jimmie Joe was frozen in the memories that had framed the first eight years of his life, and his attitude went beyond ingrained patterns to clear determination not to be weaned to strange and hostile ways. You could watch him eat with knife and fork or lace his shoes or otherwise practice the new habits he had easily learned, and yet know damned well that at the first pretext he would slough them like a snake's outworn skin. He was not an outgoing sort of youngster, moreover, just as Vetch, who was bending his reserved nature to breaking, was not a particularly outgoing man.

The baby was a constant worry, for the ailing little one was the one aspect of his new family that found a spot of undiluted warmth in Sam Vetch. The infant came quickly to know him, to smile at the sound of his voice, to clasp his playful finger; yet little Carl rarely made a noise of approbation or any sound except for a sob or a cough. Vetch knew with a dismal certainty that he could not live in this condition indefinitely, that improvement must come soon or never. They had consulted doctors about Carl's condition in every sizable town through which they had passed coming here; none could offer more than vague diagnoses that rarely agreed.

Sara herself began to manifest odd symptoms that made him realize that much of her apparent composure was superficial. All her courage could not mask the scars she had not wanted him to see. Her withholding as a woman was part of that scarring legacy; so were the dreams. She had mentioned how Neeta, her erstwhile sister-in-law, had beat her with a stick, and she lived those times over and over in her dreams— these and other memories that she may have endured stoically when they had occurred found a violent and vocal expression when she slept: her guards were down. Vetch had the devil's own time restraining her during these nightmares, which always woke the baby and set him crying. Here again it seemed that time, which should have made some alleviation, was having little or no good effect.

But one evening, by dropping a chance and joshing remark, he got a strong and unexpected whiff of the truth. What he jokingly said was, "Still worried that your other husband might show up?"

She was momentarily too startled to hide the haunted strain behind her face; she was carrying dirty dishes to the wash pan and, when she set them down, dropped and broke a plate. As he helped her gather up the shattered fragments of china Vetch noticed that her hands were trembling.

About to remonstrate, he thought better of it. Years of association with the army, where combat and fear went arm in arm, had taught him by observation that fear was not a matter to be reasoned away. Skeptical himself, he did not have the words to argue her out of what still seemed to him an irrational fantasy.

Late the following afternoon he and Hilario and Ned Coombs were coming in after a day of winnowing out and applying blab boards to slow-weaning calves so their mothers would have a chance to regain their strength. As they rode down the last approach of piney slope above the headquarters Vetch spotted a strange horse, a white-stockinged bay, tethered at the tie rail in front of the house. Seeing that the animal was equipped after the Indian fashion caused a breath of sudden fear to clot in his throat. Without a word he touched spurs to his pinto, and, coming fast off the slope, veered into the trampled yard.

Starting to swing to the ground, he heard from the open door Sara's quiet laugh. He finished his dismount slowly and started for the porch, only to halt in total astonishment as a man lounged into the doorway with an easy, remembered grace.

"How you doing, Sam?" Nick Tana said negligently, holding out a hard brown hand.

At some other time in his life Vetch might conceivably have been happier to see someone, but he could not remember when. He introduced Nick to Hilario and Ned Coombs as they rode up curiously. Old Ned had his look and promptly reined off toward the corral, muttering that first it was greasers and then pint-sized breeds and all that had been wanting was a full-growed one. Hilario, with his usual dark-faced reserve, gave a civil word and handshake before following Ned.

Nick said quizzically, as he preceded Vetch into the house, "Something eating on that old fella?"

"Nothing he ain't too old to get over," Vetch said. "Nick, you had to come this far for a reason, and I am blamed curious."

Nick slacked back into his chair and picked up his half-empty cup, which Sara now freshened from the coffeepot bubbling on the stove. A little pleased smile curved her lips, and Jimmie Joe had drawn up a chair close by the visitor. Nick had obviously brought something long needed to this roof; his brash humor had livened, at least temporarily, the cold gloom

133

that had been thickening like a shell around the whole household.

"Things been pretty quiet since the army hazed Toriano and the others onto San Carlos," Nick said, and lifted his cup in idle salute. "Anyway, the old game wasn't the same without you, chief. So I came up here like you said. Use another hand?"

Vetch picked up the cup Sara had filled for him. "You was on before you asked." He sipped his coffee and set the cup down, saying mildly, "Nick, there has to be more to it than that."

"How you figure?"

"Scouting was made to suit for you, and a cow job ain't. You had a life for yourself back there and plenty of friends—"

"None better than I got here," Nick parried.

"No, but a sight more of them. And I don't reckon you acquired any sudden affection for cows."

Nick glanced at the boy and mildly admonished him in Apache. Jimmie Joe scowled openly, and then Sara said sharply, "Do as you're told. Go and tend the horses."

The boy went out with lagging steps, fully aware that they were about to discuss matters not for his ears and therefore interesting. Nick dug out his wallet and produced a folded newspaper clipping that he handed to Vetch, saying meagerly, "That there is three-weeks-old news." Sara, wiping her hands on her apron, came up behind Vetch's chair and read over his shoulder.

Vetch raised a stunned, angry gaze, dropping the clipping on the table. "That's a hell of a thing," he said heavily. "No sense to it. A man like—"

Sara made a soft sound in her throat, and he felt her hand grip his chair back. "A Sharps rifle," she whispered. "A Sharps rifle."

Nick Tana nodded, his dark face wooden and somber. "There's sense all right, Sam. There were two men shot a 'Pache named Susto that night we caught up with Toriano's women and children in Crenna Canyon. Now one of them men is dead. Sergeant Patrick Rudabaugh." His black eyes, hard and sharp as obsidian, turned on Sara Vetch. "Ma'am, this Susto. He was your brother-in-law, wasn't he, and not your husband?"

"Yes," Sara said tonelessly. "I have told Sam all of the truth, Mr. Tana."

"About Salvaje?"

"All of it."

Nick said mildly, "All right," and looked back at Vetch. "I sounded out my ma's kin at San Carlos and picked up enough here and there to build on what I'd already guessed. That was before Sarge Rudabaugh was killed. Then I guessed at a lot more."

Vetch was beginning to understand. "You're still guessing." He tapped the clipping with a blunt forefinger. "All this news piece says was that Sergeant Rudabaugh was found dead and scalped by the road between Fort Sutro and Ocotillo one morning after he spent a night drinking in town. A couple night sentries at the fort claim they heard a shot shortly after midnight, and it sounded like a Sharps rifle."

"What it don't say," Nick observed, "is that every scout at Sutro, me included, was out hunting for track of the sergeant's killer. We never found a sign. But what I got in mind is that Salvaje is known to carry a Sharps buffalo rifle—a special sort of Sharps. One of Toriano's bucks I talked to said that Salvaje took this gun years ago off a rich Mexican *haciendado* he killed. This Mex fella must of had the gun crafted for his own sporting use. You know there was not over two thousand of them Sharps made—with the buffalo gone and all the repeaters in use today, you don't see many of them old buffalo guns. But for range and accuracy a good Sharps can still shoot rings around any other rifle ever made."

"He was very attached to that rifle." Sara's quiet voice was marked by a mounting tension. "He would spend hours cleaning and oiling it. He saved his cartridge cases and made his own bullets, but he always needed bar lead and powder and primers—he would kill and ransack just on the off chance of finding some. That must be why he killed that Stack family—his enemies, as he considered enemies, were always Mexicans, not Anglos. He would practice constantly with his gun; his marksmanship was uncanny."

Nick nodded soberly, saying, "That Sharps gives him quite a reach too," and looked squarely at Vetch. "Maybe even as far as here, Sam. If he knew about Rudabaugh, he must know about the other man who shot his brother."

"But how?"

"From Neeta," Sara said quickly, and at Nick's questioning look added, "my sister-in-law, Susto's wife. He would have followed our trail to Crenna Canyon where the troop overtook us, and would know that the captured women and children were sent to San Carlos. If he found Neeta there she could, and I'm sure would, have told him everything. She was present when Sam and the sergeant shot her husband."

Nick said pointedly, "Then I'm guessing he knows all he needs to know. Hell, I mentioned to my own kin on reservation that the white scout Vetch had married the white woman from Toriano's band and taken her and the two half-Apache kids to New Mexico. Why not? Makes a good story, the kind folks red or white will pass along for years. Yes, sir, I reckon Salvaje knows."

The blood had drained from Sara's face; she swayed unsteadily and placed both palms flat on the table, leaning there. "Salvaje," she said and paused, reaching for a semblance of calm. "Salvaje cared about three things that I am sure of. His rifle—killing Mexicans—and his blood relations. Susto and his two sons were his last living kin."

The dead certainty of both Sara and Nick was

impressive, and so was the fact that Nick had come this far way to give warning. To Vetch, this whole business had a tinge of sweeping unreality that his phlegmatic mind could not take in all at once. But his gaze dropped again to the soiled clipping before him, an undeniable statement of Sergeant Rudabaugh's seemingly wanton death at the hands of an unknown assassin. What kind of killer would patiently wait on a night road to drop his victim with a rifle made for long-range, not the point-blank shooting that darkness would make necessary?

Thinking further, Vetch felt his spine crawl as he considered the days and nights of patient vigil that had given the killer knowledge of which of the many Sutro troopers was Rudabaugh. He must have prowled about and inside even the fort itself, waiting and spying and listening, sifting the fragments seen and overheard into a cohesive meaning that would enable him to identify his quarry and earmark his habits, his comings and goings, for the ideal moment when he paid the score for the dead Susto. The whole maneuver would have required an uncanny, almost unthinkable stealth and craft, yet so it must have been done. A single question now to Sara brought the reply that yes, Salvaje understood English well enough.

All that, Vetch thought incredulously, *for a brother he never saw much . . .*

With that thought, he had a chill understanding of the deeper reason behind Nick's concern and Sara's white-faced fear. Considering Rudabaugh's fate, there was excellent reason for believing that Salvaje could and would in his good time find his way even to a remote mountain ranch if his goal were the second killer of his brother. But before now, Sara had pounced with a mother's instinct on the one element that would provide yet a more powerful motive to a father: his sons, his last human ties, were here.

Sara, looking at him with agonized eyes, read his understanding; she whispered, "Oh God, no. It can't happen. He can't have them."

Nick's mystified glance slid from one to the other, and Vetch said, "She means the kids," and flatly then: "He won't get them." He pushed to his feet. "Nick, I'm mighty grateful."

"Came to offer my services too. You'll need all the help you can get, chief."

"I expect so," Vetch said, adding with a residue of skepticism, "if he comes. I ain't going to stampede, but I'll feel a sight better with you around to read the sign. He hesitated. "Nick, this is a mighty big thing for a man to do."

The corners of Nick's wide mouth upturned in a smile that hinted at irony. "I got to lay this out cold turkey, Sam. Being part white, I might all things equal feel more kindly toward God's chosen race if it wasn't for a breed's lot." Something quivered nakedly, momentarily, in his eyes. "Them boys wouldn't lose a thing for going with Salvaje. Beg your pardon, Miss Sara, but it's so. He would take them down to the Madre maybe and raise them wild and teach them to kill Mexes, but they will face a sight worse here, to my way of thinking."

Sara bit her underlip, and her eyes smoldered. "Exactly why did you come here then, Mr. Tana?"

Nick lowered his eyes to his cup, and his hands cradling it squeezed enough to make the veins stand out. "I could fancy up fit to kill in a white man's duds, and all the pure-quill white folks would still look at me and see a bare-butt siwash dancin' around a fire. Maybe they can't rightly help themselves; I don't know enough to judge. But I know that Sam Vetch is one white man who looks at any man and don't see but a man. In my case he seen a man he liked, and he didn't need to stop and dig out his Sunday-go-to-meetin' notions before he knew it. He just knew, like I did, and we neither of us ever felt required to say so. Maybe that don't sound like much. I tell you it's a hell of a lot."

Even as he ceased talking Nick was coming in that lithe motion to his feet, and, not looking at either of them, turned and walked noiselessly out the door.

Vetch sat where he was, hearing Nick lead his horse away to the corral. Presently Sara moved with a stifled sigh toward the stove, and he glanced at her. "Don't be fretting about this. Nick and me have worked tandem before. What one of us misses in sign the other will generally find."

The Stalking Moon

Worry lay like an indefinable stain across her expression. "I—wish it were possible to leave here."

"Leave?" He stared at her, the idea not having remotely occurred before now. "This is our home. We ain't leaving it for anything."

"I mean for a while, until—"

"Leave!" He broke in on her speech with a small anger. "No, sir, not ever. We ain't running and we ain't being drove out, either." He came to his feet and stalked out to the porch; he halted, scowling, and fumbled for his pipe.

Part of his reaction was the simple, defensive stubbornness of a man who had earned his roots the hard way and whose feeling for them, once they were sunk, verged on an obsession. He had only to think of the years and dreams and sweat that had gone into the concreteness of realization. Even if Sara's anxiety were understandable, he could not help feeling a nudge of disappointment in her. He would have thought that she had come to share in her own way some part of his deep feeling for this place, a kind of pride that was indistinguishable from family interest.

The irritation settled in the back of his mind like a nettling gadfly and stayed there through supper and into the evening, which was saturated with a general atmosphere of bitter unrest. Jimmie Joe, as if sensing the infusion of a fresh tension of which they chose to keep him ignorant, gave several displays of sullen rebellion that brought Vetch to the edge of punishing him. He had always avoided any physical action that could only deepen the rift between himself and the boy.

Little Carl, meanwhile, had developed a particularly bad cough, possibly from the heavy dampness in the air; even the night chill had not lifted the oppressive humidity. Sara, constantly hovering around him, thought he was running a fever. Vetch, watching the play of heat lightning over the dark peaks, allowed that it was only the temperature, which would fall when the rain did.

The storm broke soon afterward. A high wind dipped off the lofty sierras and drove leadlike clouds before it, and shortly solid sheets of water were rattling on roof and windows, which trembled to the continuous, massive reverberations of thunder.

Vetch sat in the parlor and tried to concentrate on his stockman's journal, but Nick's coming and the news he had brought, the residues of embattled irritation, the long-building stress of angry frustrations, filled him with a restless, acrid bitterness. He doused the lamp and went to the master bedroom. The baby was seemingly restful now, and Sara sat by the Adamesque mirror, brushing her hair. She was in camisole and skirt, having removed her blouse, and when she briefly met his gaze in the glass, there was a trace of self-consciousness in the way she averted her eyes.

The Stalking Moon

She bore little resemblance now to the bony, weather-beaten Apache captive she had been. A few more years of that grueling life would have broken her physically, but at this point the resources demanded by pure survival had left her with a glow of amazing strength and energy that would last all her life. Her narrow features were not pretty and never would be, but they were regular enough and suited her filled-out face better. The former matted dullness of her thick chestnut hair had yielded to daily care so that it had a rich, crackling gloss under the brisk long strokes of the brush. The dark rough stain of weather had gradually faded and smoothed so that the soft press of lamplight made a tawny satin of her face and bare arms and shoulders. The sturdy body had fleshed out with a robust fullness of maturity at last permitted to assert itself, for she had been little more than a girl when captured. Her large breasts were firm and proud; they strained insistently at the low camisole and swelled above it in two branching shadowed arcs. He had not seen her like this before, and he felt the subtle perspiration break along his temples and the slow pulse hammer of his blood, and then, like a taste of brass on his tongue, the rise of the brute hunger that lay in the gentlest of men.

She had laid aside the brush; her quick fingers made three thick strands of her hair to plait them in the habitual heavy braid she wore to sleep. And he said in a voice that was guttural and almost ugly, "Leave it that way."

She came half around on the stool and her eyes went wide and startled; they darkened strangely, and he thought this was fear. The baby's voice lifted in a low, keening sound, and something in it wiped Vetch's mind blank. The cry dissolved at once into a retching, sucking sound that was unlike any of the infant's coughing fits till now.

Sara brushed past him with a muffled cry and scooped up the baby. "Sam, oh, Sam, he is choking!"

"A touch of the grippe," Vetch said. "It happens in this weather."

Sara rocked the infant in her arms, crooning to him in the familiar half chant. Vetch came over and peered at him, touching the smooth cheek, which had a dry hot texture. His eyes were shut while the tiny fingers clutched blindly, spasmodically, at the air, and suddenly Vetch realized that he was actually sobbing for breath.

"Oh, Sam, he *is* choking!"

Vetch was already yanking on his slicker as he told her to burn sulfur and keep the baby warm. Then he was dashing from the house across the drenched yard to the stable. Throwing saddle and bridle on his pinto, he had the impression of behaving like a man without a minute to lose. That thought, as he tightened the cinch, wrenched a grunt of brittle despair from him. With the nearest doctor a good twenty miles away, facing hours of riding out a stormy night there and back along a wilderness trail clogged by timber and brush and stony hills, a man counting an extra minute was a man grasping at a straw in the wind.

Chapter Eleven

There was a young eternity of pressing through wind-lashed torrents of icy rain till all his flesh was numbed by the wet cold working beneath his slicker; he could no longer feel his knees urging the horse's flanks. His fingers around the reins seemed blocky and frozen. Equally numb, his senses were dazzled by the writhing white snakes of lightning and the sullen cannonade of steady thunder. Not willing to pause for his own sake, not daring to pause for the horse's, Vetch drove the stumbling animal relentlessly on.

Then he was plunging down the muddy channel of Spanish Crossing's street; he was hammering at Dr. Sykes's door and rousing him out and saying to get his clothes on. Not waiting, Vetch then slogged through the heavy mud, leading the pinto to the livery barn, which was closed at this hour. Vetch did not hesitate; with unfeeling hands he unbarred the big double doors and led his mount inside. By the time the doctor arrived Vetch had the two fresh animals saddled and bridled.

Early on the return ride the storm mercifully lost violence; the rain slackened to a gentle misery of slow drizzle while the wind held bearably low and was at their backs. Even the thunder was so intermittent that Vetch's tired ears registered every syllable of the doctor's steady cursing. Vetch had ridden out the full brunt of the storm and had enjoyed not a moment to thaw out; by the time they reached the ranch he could only collapse into the leather armchair by the fireplace, where Sara had laid a roaring fire. The doctor bustled on into the bedroom.

As a slow restoration of feeling and sensory impression came, Vetch heard the low onrun of Sara's and the doctor's voices, but they ran together in a meaningless jumble. His head ached and his eyelids felt like crusty lead; the fire's hot aura ate soporifically into his consciousness, and so—*Just for a minute now*—he let his eyes close.

He became aware of a hand rough on his arm; then he was on his feet with a start, facing Dr. Sykes. He saw the changed expression on Sykes's irascible face, and he knew even before the doctor said in a remarkably soft tone, "I'm sorry, Mr. Vetch. Deeply sorry."

Long minutes passed after Sykes took his leave, and still Vetch could not nerve himself to enter the bedroom. He had not heard a whisper of sound from there. *She is a woman like other women; she could cry or whoop or anything but this.* Then he heard it, a sound that he knew and yet could not give credence to; the short hairs rose at the back of his neck.

The blood in his veins was cold; he stalked through the rooms and halted in the bedroom doorway. She was kneeling before the rude box crib, swaying her head and shoulders; she shook the unbound mass of her hair, and on her lips was a loose singsong chant. He had heard Apache women wail for their dead; he knew. Beyond his will, the breath gathered in his lungs and a savage, silencing order raged from his throat. She stopped at once; her chin settled gradually to her chest.

Vetch wheeled and strode through the rooms out to the porch; he let the damp chill night cool the cursing fever of his thoughts. Grief was right; grief was good, but there would be none of that kind, by God, under this roof.

He slept on the parlor settee that night. When false dawn broke, something—he was not sure what—brought him awake. He eased to the bedroom and softly opened the door and saw that Sara was not there. Though her clothes were scattered about the room, the bed had not been slept in. Vetch started through the rooms toward the rear of the house, calling her name, only to stop dead at the kitchen threshold.

She was squatting on the rough floor, hugging her knees. She was clad in only a camisole, the skirt bunched back off her thighs, which were drawn up against her breasts. Her naked legs and arms were clotted with blood from a score of deep gashes which had streamed down her flanks and stained the single garment. The big butcher knife, its blade eloquently tarnished with a slick blackness, lay by her feet. Her head was thrown back, eyes shut, and the muscles of her arched throat quivered—she made no noise at all.

This time he did not shout, for there was no emotion in him that resembled anger. He raised her to her feet, talking quietly the while, and looked at the doorway. Jimmie Joe, roused by his voice, stood there regarding his mother's condition with a mingled anger and fear. Vetch was in no humor for tolerating his feisty bristling, and he snapped at the boy to fetch some stovewood. Something in his tone sent Jimmie Joe scurrying. Vetch stoked the big range and got water boiling. She was passive as the cuts were cleansed and bandaged, and afterward she was put to bed.

Vetch went to the cook shack where Ned and Hilario and Nick were preparing breakfast, quietly told what had happened, and barely acknowledging their sympathy, of which even old Ned Coombs had a gruff word, gave them their work orders. Today Vetch did not accompany them; he stayed in the house all day and rarely left Sara's side. She lay motionless with her eyes fixed on the ceiling and seemed not to hear when he spoke. Now and then, always with gentle patience, he tried again; by nightfall he provoked a short reply in asking whether she would eat now; she said no. He talked some more, never pressing her, and finally her eyes closed: she slept.

The next morning when he awoke Sara was already up, matter-of-factly going about her accustomed work, but never speaking unless spoken to first. At mid-morning they held a rough service by the baby's grave on the granite west slope above the ranch headquarters. The men stood awkwardly by, their heads uncovered, while Vetch said a few words and an amen. Sara's eyes were dry and distant; her hands held tightly the shoulders of Jimmie Joe, whose face was brown smooth stone, holding him as if to reassure herself that the son remaining to her was here and safe.

Life went on as usual, except that the house seemed inordinately still and empty. The dry, frequent coughing of the baby had never depressed Sam Vetch nearly as much as his awareness of that sick small life being no more; he had not realized how those feeble little fingers would prove finally strong in their hold on him. For several days in order to keep a watchful eye on Sara, he found ways to busy himself about the place. But having done a single violence of blind bereavement on herself, she acted with a mechanical normalcy except for her unspeaking apathy.

Vetch waited out the days, unflagging in his gentleness and small considerations to her. But as time went on and she showed no outward hint of alleviated grief he felt—not anger—but a nonplussed sadness growing heavily in him. Because this state of affairs could not continue, he found himself speaking bluntly one night as they prepared for bed.

"Patience don't come as hard to me as to some, but it's been two weeks now. If nothing else, you might find a civil word."

Her hand, brushing down the sleek dark chestnut fall of her unbound hair as she sat by the mirror, halted the even strokes. Her eyes came around and up. "More than that," she whispered. "I—I have not known how to say it. But I have wanted to, Sam."

"Say what?"

"That I liked you from the first." She paused, moistening her lips. "I mean from the time you first found us and helped us. I liked you more than I could believe I had any right to. But after we were married, I could not forget why you had made the bargain. Oh, Sam, I could have forgotten everything that had gone before—everything—if not for that." She came to her feet, a little unsteadily; the half-healed scars on her arms were plain beneath the light. "I have had the feeling that you've blamed yourself about Carl."

"We are settled too far from a doctor."

She shook her head with a quick vehemence. "The doctors could do nothing before, and neither of us could have guessed how quickly it would come. And no man could have done more than you tried to do, Sam." Her words dropping to a husky whisper ended; her fingers unclasped the brush and it clattered on the little table, and she came across the room to him.

Quite suddenly and with a continuous sense of surprise, Sam Vetch was learning that life could be very good. For Sara, her bad dreams were ended as her new present eroded the past into forgetfulness. For both of them it was an awakening to a new wonder that the daily trials of living could not dim.

But in growing apart from her dark memories, Sara began gradually to lose something more. Her hold on Jimmie Joe, strong-bred of familiarity, was becoming tenuous and uncertain with every passing day. The boy had only a few recollections of his savage father, vivid though they were, and so Sara's influence had remained dominant. Now, sensing with an awareness beyond any spoken declaration that his mother had returned to the hostile white world in mind as well as body, he slowly extended his patterns of resentment to her, while his hatred of Vetch, always low-smoldering, grew to open sullen rebellion. Twice Vetch caught him torturing small animals, a rabbit he had snared and then a squirrel, and the second time he threatened punishment. He had the bleak feeling that time would never accomplish for Jimmie Joe what it had for Sara. If anything, the boy was retreating deeper into the primitive ways that had been his first birthright.

With plenty of domestic responsibilities and the hard measure of his daily work to fill his attention, Vetch almost forgot the uneasy threat that had brought Nick Tana all this way; at least he relegated the matter to the background of his mind. It was nearly a month after Nick's arrival at the ranch when, one day as he and the half-breed were packing rock salt to a high pasture, he raised the question.

The two of them had finished their task and were resting on their hunkers in the mottled shade of a big pine. Vetch said: "You seemed almighty sure that Salvaje would come."

"Well, no," Nick said around the straw he was chewing, and his tone was dry. "Not one-hundred-per-cent sure. But I'll take them ninety-ten odds any time."

"He's had time."

"You think he don't need time? Hell, man. Ask yourself how long it would take you if you was a lone man trying to locate a dinky backwoods ranch through strange country full of enemies, with just a sketchy knowledge of the language and you can't ask directions. Besides"—Nick restored the straw to his strong square teeth, which appeared to half smile as he considered the sky—"besides, he is Injun and has got all time in the world. If he don't find you this year, then the next. Don't be in no hurry, chief, because you can lay odds he ain't."

Vetch made a wry face, and then Nick said abruptly, "Get a dog."

"What's that?"

"You plan on going to Spanish Crossing for supplies tomorrow. All right, there ought to be a cur or two around town someone will let you take off their hands for nothing much. A good dog will always pick up what a man misses."

Vetch decided that if nothing else he would sleep a good deal sounder for following up the suggestion.

Late that afternoon, as they rode in and dismounted by the corral, Sara came out of the house holding a sullen Jimmie Joe by the arm. Her lips were compressed to a fine line, always a hint of her well-bridled temper. "Sam. I caught him doing it again. A squirrel he snared. He— Never mind."

Without a word Vetch reached for his belt, but Nick put out his hand. "That won't do. There shouldn't be no need with an Injun kid."

"There's a need now."

"All right, but that is the wrong way." Nick took the boy by the collar and shook him, but not roughly. "Your pa has told you it is bad to kill them animals slow."

The boy looked ready to spit; he said in Apache, "The white-eyes is not my father."

Without more ado Nick lifted him onto his toes and propelled him at a fast walk across the yard and out of sight behind the barn. By the time Vetch and Sara had come around the corner, Nick, kneeling on the creek bank, had plunged the boy's head into the icy roiling water. Jimmie Joe was thrashing wildly, and then not so wildly.

"That's enough!" Sara cried.

Nick grunted, "Let's hope so," and hauled the boy out, dumping him face down on the bank. His wiry frame heaved spasmodically; he coughed and gagged, and was too dizzy to rise. Nick watched him a placid moment, then said, "That's why there's never a need to punish Injun kids. But you are trying to knock out what is second nature to him. He was raised on deviling little critters."

"That ain't why he does it," Vetch snapped. "It spites me, is why."

"Sure, but my point is he don't see no wrong to it. Or in spiting you either. A man spites his enemy any ways he can."

Nick's blunt summing up was as accurate as it was unsparing, Vetch knew, but as badly as he wanted to break through the boy's shell, he had a cautious sense that physical threats or punishment were not the way. The boy might understand the meaning of discipline as inflicted by a friend or a blood relation, but how could he react to it from one he hated except by more hatred? Yet pretending to ignore him was not the answer either, and Vetch decided with a sudden conviction that he had not really been trying with the boy.

After briefly considering this, he abruptly said that he would take Jimmie Joe with him to Spanish Crossing the next day. Nick glanced at the boy's sullen face and shrugged. Sara said nothing, but she looked doubtful.

Tomorrow, Vetch thought, he would be in no

hurry to reach town and conclude his business there. Darkness would catch them on the return ride; a camp under the stars had a way of working a wizardry of companionship between men and men—men and boys too. At least he could allow himself that hope. For all the outdoor jaunts he had taken the boy on, they had never camped out. This way the idea would seem casual, not forced.

At sunup, after finishing breakfast, Vetch went to the corral where the crew, as was the custom, waited for the day's orders. Vetch outlined their duties for the day and through the next day while they saddled up. He cinched rigs on mounts for himself and the boy, filled the saddlebags with a few provisions, and selected a third horse to serve as pack beast on the return trip. Then he beckoned Nick Tana off to one side.

"Nick, it's as well if one man stays close to the place while I'm gone. And keep a good eye peeled. Understand?"

Nick nodded readily. "I figured why you only gave me jobs that will keep me on the place. I'll stick like a burr, don't worry."

Shortly Vetch and Jimmie Joe headed east from the ranch. Vetch rode slowly, enjoying the dew-fresh coolness of the morning. Jimmie Joe led the pack horse as Vetch had directed him, always holding an aloof distance to the rear. The boy was as sullen and withdrawn as Vetch had ever seen him, but since he had not expected to effect a change in a day or even overnight he paid it little attention.

They came into town by mid-afternoon. This being Saturday, Spanish Crossing was animated by a mild traffic that was at its never-bustling peak. The place was a freight stop on the only route through a looming arm of mountains, a stopover for the occasional horsebacker traveling through, and a supply post for chance drifters, trappers, prospectors, and a sprinkling of high-country ranchers near and far, which totaled up to a slight need.

After sweeping an eye over the handful of people he saw, a couple of ranch families and several cowhands, Vetch hesitated only briefly before leaving Jimmie Joe to his own devices, not even admonishing him to stay out of trouble.

Tramping into the general store, Vetch unfolded his lengthy list of needs and handed it to the storekeeper, who, as he cheerily filled it, kept up a running spiel of range-country and trail gossip. Vetch was not very interested, and little more so by the man's declaration that, no sir, he didn't see the right of some folks' calling a fellow a squaw man just because. It was apparent that word had already gone the rounds. Knowing the wildfire way of all small talk in this lonely and news-hungry country, Vetch did not really blame people for not minding their own business, but those like this storekeeper who wore their liberalism like badges rubbed against his grain.

It was the man's sudden veering to another

matter that brought Vetch, half listening as he inspected the gun display case, to attention. "What was that you said?"

"Why, a grub-line drifter who hit town last night was talking in the saloon," the storekeeper said, consulting the list and then reaching to a high shelf for bottles of Dr. Robertson's Stomach Elixir and Dr. Godbold's Vegetable Balsam of Life and other patent medicines that old Ned Coombs was dead sure kept his body and soul in one piece. "Must of been a sight to see, way he needed the whisky. Says he come on the ranch high noon yesterday and hallooed, hoping someone would say to light down. No answer, but the door was open and he got curious. Terrible thing. The whole family murdered, all the Ortegas. Pa, mother, two half-growed boys, a young girl, and a baby. Two bodies in the back yard, man and one of the boys, had their heads shot apart while they was splitting wood. Must of been a big-bore gun. The others was caught inside, and they was plain butchered. Terrible thing."

The storekeeper set the bottles on the counter, frowning, shaking his gray head, and Vetch said, hearing the harsh and unnatural tautness of his own voice, "Ortega—Mexicans?"

"Only Mexican fambly hereabouts—that is, who run their own outfit. Well, this traveling man did not stay around to bury anyone, so some of the townfolks rode out there this morning." The storekeeper tongued his cheek. "Seems 'most like Injun work, all that killing for nothing at all that a man could see. Except that no Apaches never swung this far northeast more than a few times I know of, even in the old days, and we never had Injun trouble outside of then. Besides, these folks was all killed clean as a whistle, no torture. The funny thing—all of them down to the baby in the crib was scalped. That ain't like an Apache's work, though, is it?"

"A few Apaches maybe," Vetch said mechanically. "They never got onto the habit much."

"Well, I call it pretty terrible. Why, the Ortega place is on Little Creek, which ain't over three hours' ride from here. Gives a man the willies, mostly if he has a wife and young ones. A lot of fellows will be keeping guns by their pillows and sleeping light for a time to come, I tell you."

Three hours, Vetch thought, *and that was yesterday*. There was not a jot of doubt in his mind. "Get all them things together, will you? I am in a hurry."

This was, in spite of his previous plans, no exaggeration; quite suddenly Sam Vetch was in a sweating rush to return home.

Chapter Twelve

While he was diamond-hitching the load of supplies on the packhorse he had brought, Vetch became aware of a small commotion downstreet. Glancing that way, he saw two boyish figures tumbling about in the moiling dust in front of the livery barn. With a sigh Vetch finished the hitch and stepped around the horse's rump, and went down the street, not hurrying.

As he came up, Tom Dodd, the stableman, stepped frowning from the runway. "You plan on stopping it, Vetch?"

Vetch moved his head in negation, and Dodd seemed satisfied. At the moment, as his son and Jimmie Joe rolled and clinched in the dust, young Matt Dodd was gaining the upper hand. He was several years the half-breed boy's elder, with a large advantage in height and heft. Now he succeeded in coming atop Jimmie Joe and solidly straddling him, his weight immobilizing the small wiry body.

Vetch, though he would not have interfered in any case, knew that, despite the apparent inequity of the tussle, there might still come a jolting reversal. Indian youths were exposed from earliest childhood to rough-and-tumble wrestling, and he guessed that Jimmie Joe had so far lacked only opportunity in this close-quarter engagement. Nor was he wrong.

With a writhing heave now, Jimmie Joe succeeded finally in dislodging his bigger opponent and squirming free of him. In almost the same instant the smaller boy was on his feet, braced and poised for Matt's next move. Matt scrambled up belatedly and charged at once. Jimmie Joe sidestepped in a motion of fluid ease, and with a quick wrist grip and a sly foot sent Matt tumbling in the dust. He would not let Matt close with him again, but simply accepted the bigger boy's bullish charges, converting Matt's own momentum with slight variations on a few basic grips and throwing him each time. When Matt lay on his back dusty and panting, unable to rise again, Jimmie Joe straddled him and wickedly pummeled his face and ribs.

Tom Dodd tried to interfere then, and Vetch blocked him. "Not yet, Tom. You wanted this."

The stableman came to an uncertain halt, but a few seconds later he burst out, "For God's sake, that's enough!"

Young Matt's nose and face were being cut to

ribbons by a brittle tattoo of small bony fists, and Vetch reached down now and peeled Jimmie Joe off his adversary as he might peel away an agitated leech. Though the boy ceased all resistance as soon as he was set on his feet, Vetch held onto him with a big hand gently wrapped around his neck.

Matt got up by himself, looking foolish, but then stuck out his hand readily. "You licked me square, boy. I got no grudge."

Jimmie Joe pursed his lips and spat neatly in Matt's outstretched palm. Vetch started to give him an angry shake, but let it go with a growled word that ordered Jimmie Joe back to the horses.

Vetch remembered Nick's suggestion. Despite the overriding sense of urgency accompanying his new, certain knowledge of the danger close on them all, he could spare the few minutes needed for this errand.

Actually he was less than fifteen minutes in locating a likely dog and closing the deal. A question to the storekeeper elicited the information that the local saloon man had a stray mutt he had taken to feeding. The saloonkeeper was happy to turn the animal, a husky yellow dog scarred by age and vicissitude, over to Vetch, refusing payment. With the dog tethered to the packhorse by a length of rope, they left town as the afternoon shadows lengthened on the slopes and flats.

In the anxiety of knowing that anything might have happened during his absence, Vetch pushed for a fast return to the ranch. But twenty miles of rugged and brush-clogged country held down their progress, and after his own horse took a bad spill Vetch clamped down on his feelings and held to a moderate pace. Sunset and twilight seemed to press with unseasonable swiftness across the high country tonight (all in his mind, he knew, chafing with restraint), and the coming of solid, unrelieved darkness forced an early halt.

They were still a good six miles from the ranch, but to forge through a moonless night along a barely defined trail on this kind of terrain was a difficult proposition. Therefore Vetch matter-of-factly bivouacked at the halt and brusquely set the boy to camp tasks. There was no frantic note in his admitted concern, since Nick Tana could be trusted to keep a sound lookout for the least sign of trouble. False dawn would provide enough light to move on, and they would be home by sunrise. Meantime no Apache would stir abroad by dark. But he reminded himself, *This one runs by his own rules*, and was uneasy again. Knowing what little he did of the man called Salvaje, he could only chafe at any delay.

They squatted on either side of a compact blaze and ate the beans and bacon Vetch cooked. The rosy flames polished the boy's smooth thin face with a coppery, shifting glow, and, studying him, Vetch tried to read his thoughts. The boy ate stolidly and slowly, relaxed and totally unconcerned. It was as though the fight and his victory had released his hostile tensions; now he was merely indifferent and mildly sleepy.

An odd sound from among the firelit boles of the giant pines enclosing the little clearing, their boughs arching to a ragged blackness overhead, brought the boy alert. He quit eating and cocked his head. To Vetch that sound had been the stuttering low hoot of an ordinary owl; when it came again the boy's slight frame stiffened perceptibly.

Before Vetch realized it, all his senses had begun to strain at hair trigger and quest for some alien quality among the familiar patterns of the night. He caught himself and glanced with quick suspicion at the boy. Jimmie Joe listened intently, his black-pebble eyes inscrutable with distance. He ignored Vetch.

The dog, leashed to a tree, whined in his throat and paced back and forth. But he did not bristle or growl, only watched the pair of them as if aroused by their attitudes. Narrowly eying the boy, Vetch thought, *He is trying to get under my hide is all; he's bluffing*. That had to be it, since he had not spoken a word to the boy about his blood father's being in the vicinity, and there was no particular reason to attach significance to the common hoot of a hunting owl.

How do you know there ain't? How can you tell what signals he might have been learned? A moment later Vetch thought angrily, *Hell, even if he had never overheard Sara and me talking, which he might have, he could of guessed the*

165

truth from just how we acted now and again.

The eerie flutter of owl noise came once more, and abruptly Jimmie Joe ceased to listen. Seeming wholly satisfied by what he had heard, he scraped up his plate; a shadow of a smile flitted across his dark cheeks as he laid it aside. Never glancing at Vetch, he unrolled his blankets and stretched out, folding his arms beneath his head.

Judging that he was being laughed at, Vetch remained uncomfortably intent, but the low hoot did not come a fourth time. Was this only a handy coincidence? Granted that Jimmie Joe's father was quite probably prowling these same hills by now, even he could not locate this well-hidden fire unless he were to pass within a few yards of their campsite.

Vetch caught the boy's gaze, which was fixed on him with a steady, open mockery. Even that told nothing; whether his father were really nearby or whether the boy were amused by successfully unnerving Vetch, he would have cause to mock. For all his silent rationale, Vetch was unsettled; sweat broke along his ribs and his back muscles began to crawl. He felt a succession of near-uncontrollable impulses: to douse the fire, to withdraw into the trees, to turn at any real or fancied sound at his back. He did none of these things. He forced his muscles to unwind while he remained squatting in the bright firelight. And quite deliberately he picked up a heavy chunk of wood and tossed it on the embers; a spiral of sparks and flames danced high.

The boy had drawn a line plainly with his mocking eyes; from here on Sam Vetch must toe that line. Under no circumstances, no matter how keenly he felt the ordinary qualms of self-doubt or outright fear, he could not for an instant betray himself to the boy. Every expression and word of his would be measured by the harshest of comparisons. Only on that fierce scale of Apache standards did he stand a prayer of driving a dim wedge of first respect into a savage young mind. Even if he met the acid test of comparison, it did not remotely follow that he would win the boy's allegiance; it opened only a possibility.

The yellow dog whined softly and settled on its haunches. Looking from boy to dog, remembering the tortured little creatures, Vetch thought bitterly, *Leastways this is a full-growed dog that can outrun him. He will need to*.

Vetch settled back on his blankets, trying to compose himself for sleep that it seemed would not come. He simulated sleep and ran over a raw gamut of nocturnal fancies. He was tired; he wanted a few hours' sleep before it was light enough for travel. If the enemy were out in the trees he could do what he had come to do at any time. If he were not, no sense in bearing a freight of sleepless worry. But several hours of taut wakefulness elapsed before it seemed a fair bet that nothing would happen, and he slept.

*   *   *

He came awake with a start, and it was well past the early hour that he had intended to decamp; the gray cowl of predawn had already lifted. He roused the boy and swiftly readied the animals; a first pink welt of sunrise stung the pearly sky as they started down the trail.

It was easy in the clear morning, livened by bird song and the scolding chatter of squirrels, to discount his fears. Vetch felt a bit foolish. The boy had been quietly and cleverly baiting him last night, and so long as he chose to continue a battle for the boy's heart and mind he could expect more of the same.

The sun was high when they broke from the trees and came onto the summit of the western-most of the hills embracing the ranch head-quarters. The trail took its straggling way off a timbered bench across the hilltop and switch-backed down its long flank to the vale below. The urgent tension still held strong in Vetch, and only when he came onto the crest of the hill did the strain around his belly lift for the first time. Everything was as he had left it, familiar and quite peaceful. The morning sun gleamed on the peeled logs of the house, and a lazy thread of smoke curled from the fieldstone chimmey.

It was several seconds before his gaze, fixed on the layout, took in as a matter of dutiful course the surrounding terrain. His idle and perfunctory glance touched fleetingly the dun slope below and half registered something that snapped his eyes alert.

For a moment of sheer disbelief he could not move; then, as the meaning of the situation drove fully home, he was almost afraid to. But move he did, locking his breath in his chest and straining to make no sound as he sidled the horse backward from view of the slope.

Dropping noiselessly out of his saddle, he saw Jimmie Joe, who had fallen behind, come riding out of the trees. With a warning gesture Vetch signaled him to halt. The boy obeyed with a puzzled hesitancy. Vetch formed, "Stay here," barely moving his lips, and slipping his Winchester from its scabbard, catfooted back to the brow of the hill and stopped before reaching the drop-off. Barely letting his angle of sight top the rock-laden slant for a full view, Vetch peered downslope again, still not believing what he had seen.

A natural niche was scored flat and deep into the hillside about halfway down; it was here on the east-facing slope that Sara Vetch had chosen the gravesite of her dead infant. A rude marker of two boards nailed crosswise marked the little still-bare mound of earth.

Standing by it was a man. His back was turned and he was looking down at the grave, but what Vetch could tell about him even from here was more than enough. His black hair hung straight and long down his back, half confined by a rawhide band around his temples; he wore long leggin-moccasins of tan buckskin and a buckskin vest that left his coppery huge-thewed arms bare. A quiver of arrows and a short thick mesquite bow were slung across his back; from his shoulder, supported by a crude strap, depended a heavy rifle.

It was his size, though Sara's description had prepared Vetch for it, that was startling. The average fullblood Apache male was stocky and barrel-chested and somewhat above medium height as the tribes went. This man dwarfed them all. In the impression of bulking power that he gave, Vetch could compare him only to the big Slovak he had encountered in Silverton, and it was a bad comparison. This man was as gaunt as a great timber wolf, and the sense of something free and fierce, something that had never been tamed and would never be, reached out from his motionless stance and prickled along Vetch's spine.

With realization, a dozen questions flooded his mind, and foremost was his wonderment that the man dared expose himself on a bare slope in bold view of the ranch buildings. Yet in this moment any question was a vague undercurrent next to his topmost impulse.

He would never have another opportunity like this one, Sam Vetch knew, and the advantage was all his. It should, even considering the vagaries of downhill shooting, prove a fairly easy shot. All he had to do was inch forward the few cautious feet necessary to achieve a clear aim.

Letting his feet take each minute shift of his weight with the dainty skill of many years' training (and grateful now for every hour of it), he stepped off in painstaking silence the two yards to the position he had eye-marked. Yet he moved swiftly, and with an equal lack of waste motion brought the rifle to his shoulder. At any moment Salvaje might turn or glance around; that he had failed to mark Vetch's approach on horseback could be attributed only to his pre-occupation and the fact that a thick carpet of pine needles at the fringe of the wooden bench behind had muffled the horses' hoofs.

Quite suddenly Salvaje did move, but only to reach down and pull up the grave cross; he broke it in half with a single savage twist of his hands and tossed the pieces contemptuously aside. Once again he stood quietly, looking down.

Vetch swept the broad back with his sights and steadied them. Then the surge of revulsion; his hands felt heavy as rock. He had no illusion about the raw, total menace that the copper-skinned savage posed. Yet in this moment, through the lenses of his own manhood, Vetch saw only another man, a man grieving in the grief that is matchless: that of a father for a dead son. Appalled, he thought of killing a man on his child's grave, and a man of Vetch's sensibilities could only hesitate.

The feeling was powerful but momentary; all the stern facts that life had ingrained in him beat down the silent protest. He drew a half breath and hair fined his perspective with both eyes, sighting in.

The thin rattle of a pebble rolling downward

over the stones made a noise brittle and quite specific in the hanging stillness.

Salvaje's head swiveled around and up; his body did not otherwise move. As quickly he saw Vetch and in the same instant he was away and gone, angling down the slope in great loping bounds. It seemed impossible that so large a man could move with such noiseless and gliding quickness, like an animal or a ghost. Astonished as he was, Vetch would have fired if he could have pulled a bead on that lightning form. He could not, and then Salvaje was swallowed by a motte of trees and brush farther down the slope; he merged into the vegetation without a stir or a rustle, as if he had never been.

God, Vetch thought, feeling as if a cold fist were squeezed around his heart. And then he turned, already knowing what he would see. Jimmie Joe was not three yards behind and above him, unmoving, his small face stony and closed. As silent as Vetch himself, the boy had simply dismounted and crept forward to see what had taken his stepfather's attention—and seeing, had dislodged a single pebble with his foot, an occurrence that Vetch could be sure had been no accident.

The golden chance had come and gone; nothing he could do would change that, and there was nothing to say on the matter, except a weary, "Get on your horse," as he sheathed his rifle and stepped into the saddle. The dog gave a soft, querulous whine. Taking no chance on the boy's trying to slip away, Vetch reined over and caught up Jimmie Joe's rein.

Quite suddenly then, Vetch thought: *If he knew about the grave, he talked to somebody.* And with that, feeling the solid grip of a real fear, he spurred down the hill.

Chapter Thirteen

Vetch crossed the yard and, dropping off his pinto by the house, sent a swift glance across the silent buildings. He saw nothing of Nick or the other two hands; unless Nick had ignored his orders for some reason, something must have happened to him. The front door hung open; it creaked on a breath of wind, and Vetch let go the reins of Jimmie Joe's mount, forgetful of everything in his immediate fear. In a moment he was across the porch and inside the parlor. Finding nothing amiss there, he started across the room toward the bedroom hallway, only to come to a halt.

Sara lay on the floor, half in and half out of the corridor, her body twisted at an awkward angle against the door casing. He knelt and touched her, and when a sharp moan escaped

175

her, felt for broken bones. Assured that there were none, he gathered her up gently and carried her to the bedroom. She was dully conscious as he laid her on the quilt; a great raw bruise angled across the side of her face from hairline to throat. She did not appear otherwise injured.

She moaned; her eyes flew open and wildly quested the room. She brought the back of her hand to her cheek, wincing. "Sam—he was here."

"I know. What did he do?"

She sat upright, clutching at his arms. "Jimmie Joe!"

Vetch called to the boy, and a moment later heard his dragging steps. Jimmie Joe came sullenly to the doorway and looked at his mother's bruised face; he showed no flicker of emotion.

"Now he knows who has come," Sara whispered. "God help us!"

Vetch shook her. "What did he do?"

"He—nothing. Just this." She touched the bruise; she swung her feet to the floor and stood, moving over to her son. Taking him by the hand, she looked at Vetch. A hint of something cowed and hopeless lay in her face, and he did not like to see it.

She murmured, "He said that when he sees me again, he will cut off my nose. He is not ready yet." Vetch only nodded; that was the traditional retribution allowed the cuckolded Apache husband. "And he said to tell you something, Sam. That he is in no hurry. He said—he said that you started to die when you killed Susto, but you did not know it. You will go on dying for a time yet because he wants you to know it."

"You told him about the baby."

"How did you know?"

Vetch told her. She nodded. "Yes," and lifted the back of her hand to her cheek again. "He did not believe me when he wanted to know where Jimmie Joe was and I said with you. That was when he struck me first. Then he went out and looked at the sign around the corral. He said that the sign said I spoke true; when he was ready to leave he would take Ish-kay-nay with him to Sonora and raise him in the mountains as a boy should be raised. He hit me again, and that is all I know."

A grinding anger came to Vetch; his words were taut and even. "Where's Nick? He had orders to stay by the place."

She told him that shortly after Hilario Cortinas and Ned Coombs had left for their on-range work this morning, Hilario had come rushing back in some excitement. He had found the butchered steer up in a near pasture; the trampled earth held plenty of moccasin sign, and leading away were the tracks of an unshod pony. He had returned to the ranch to tell Nick, thinking that the half-breed might wish quickly to track down the killer of their cattle. Nick had lost no time in leaving for the pasture, after telling Hilario to remain here and keep a sharp watch. It had been a few minutes later, when

Sara had gone outside for an armload of wood, that she had been confronted silently and suddenly by Salvaje. She had called Hilario's name but got no response.

Vetch was already, as Sara finished speaking, hurrying from the house. He was less than a minute in finding Hilario. The crippled Mexican was sprawled unconscious inside the barn, a swollen welt plain at the base of his skull.

After reviving him Vetch learned that Hilario had simply entered the barn and was struck down; he had heard and seen nothing. And now Vetch was quick to describe the entire situation to him, bitterly aware that he should have done so before this. Hilario's eyes squinted almost shut as he listened. He was a native of Sonora; he knew of Salvaje, the scourge of his people. He crossed himself as he said as much.

"*Por Díos*, Sam, how was I to know? I would not have got taken by surprise if this half-breed, he had told what it was that I was to watch for. Eh?"

"I know," Vetch said. "Only that was my mistake, not Nick's. We'll be in a fight from now on, Nick and Ned and you and me. If you want to draw your pay now is the time."

Cortinas said simply, "I like this place; I will fight the fight," and ran a hand over his grayshot black hair; his teeth flashed. "I wonder that I still wear something on which to set my hat. This great killer of my people, this Salvaje—it is said he always takes their scalps."

Vetch wondered about that too; he remembered Sara's words, *He said he is in no hurry*, and wondered if this, with the sparing of Hilario's life and scalp, was part of some deadly preset pattern. And whether, if he had a more intimate knowledge of the way of that strange mind, he might gain an inkling of what to expect and how to head it off.

He told Hilario to fetch his rifle and mount guard inside the bunkhouse. From the east window a man could command a view of the whole ranch yard, and anyone coming off the circle of half-timbered hills would have to expose himself before they reached the bottom. At this moment Salvaje might well be watching from somewhere in the hill timber; if he showed himself within even a chancy range, Hilario had orders to shoot to kill.

While he was about it Vetch drove a stake into the ground by the tack-shed door and tethered the yellow dog there. Here too was a perfect vantage point. The animal would give an alarm at the first sight of a stranger, and of course for a while at all of them as well until he became accustomed to the place and its people.

Returning to the house, Vetch found Sara on the settee, her hands idle in her lap. Her eyes were apathetic. Jimmie Joe, leaning against the fireplace, gently rubbed his back along the stones; he looked like a small smug cat eying them askance with no expression. Vetch said, "Go to your room," and the boy left the parlor.

Vetch reflected that he might try to slip away and join his father. They could not watch him every minute, and there would be many chances for him to do so. Yet for a reason at which he could only guess, Vetch thought that the boy would not try to run away—not yet. He knew that his father was nearby and that Salvaje would not leave without him. He would probably wait quite passively for that moment, and meanwhile, in his savage little heart, thoroughly enjoy their discomfort.

Wearily, Vetch scaled his hat into a chair and took the settee by his wife; he watched her strong profile and had no clue to her thoughts, and presently said, "He fooled Nick and tolled him off. I guess he figured he would take a chance with a Mexican watching the place, but not a man who is half 'Pache."

She started vaguely, and only now looked at him. "Hilario isn't—"

"No. Just a crack on the head. He got caught with his back turned. No danger of that in the bunkhouse where he's on guard now. Oh, I brought home a dog too. By the shed seemed a good place to tie him." He laced his fingers together and bent his gaze to his hands, gently scowling. "I didn't want to bring this up before. It's a part of your life you could only want to be shed of. So do I. But I got to know my enemy. You know him, maybe better than anyone alive."

He felt the darkness of her gaze and when he met her eyes they fell away; her hands twisted together in little futile movements. "Not very well. Nobody did."

"Even so." Vetch paused, remembering the fate of the Ortega family two days ago; he told her about that now. "That's one thing with him, ain't it? Mexicans. Why?"

She was silent for so long that he was about to remonstrate; she said suddenly then, "Have you ever heard of the San Felipe massacre?"

He stirred his head affirmatively and thought for a moment, mustering the details. "San Felipe—village in Sonora. The governor placed a fat bounty on Apache scalps. Quite a few American tough nuts as well as Mexicans were down there hunting scalps—and they didn't much care whether the hair they lifted was Mex or Apache, seeing there wasn't much difference from the look. It got pretty bad."

Vetch leaned back against the cushions, again feeling his wife's taut gaze. He went on, "There was a band of peaceful Mimbres that used to come out of the mountains regular to trade with the Mexes in this little foothill town, San Felipe. But the old *alcalde* died, and the new one, fellow named Duro, saw a chance to make a young fortune. He caused it to be spread about that their Apache friends was about to turn on them, and when he had the people shaking in their sandals proposed his plan. They set up an old cannon at one side of the village square and loaded it with bullets and scrap iron and the like, and covered it with trade goods. Then they invited their Mimbre *compadres* to a big fiesta in the square, and when they was stuffed with food and mescal, all asleep or close to it, Duro touched off the cannon. It ripped the band to pieces—men and women and kids—and then the villagers jumped in with knives and rifle butts and finished the job. The story has it that they took close to a hundred Apache scalps."

"He was a boy of thirteen," Sara said softly. "A few escaped, and he was one. After seeing his father's face blown away. His mother on the ground screaming and clutching her entrails. His tiny sister clubbed to death by a rifle. He saw uncles and aunts and cousins . . . He ran and escaped, after snatching up his baby brother. He and a handful of others won through to their mountain camp. All agreed that they wanted revenge, but they were too few to make a fight, and this camp was no longer safe. They knew that Toriano's fighting band was a few marches north, and they decided to join him.

"He—Salvaje—knew that he must have walked with the others, carrying his brother Susto on his back for the two days and two nights it took them to find Toriano, but he had no memory of doing so. His mind seemed to have left his body. When it returned, he bent his life toward one goal: he was changed and all saw it and, believing him to be possessed, shunned him. He did not care. More and more he stayed away from the tribe, foraging alone for days, weeks at a time, driving his body to its limits and then beyond that. He was determined to become more than he was or die in the attempt. He would need strength and quickness, a craft and cunning, far beyond even his Apache fellows to carry out the destiny he had set for himself."

Sara looked down at her hands; again they made small and futile motions. "Within a few years the *alcalde*, Señor Duro, and his wife and all his children, and then, one by one, his close relatives and their families were found shot or knifed or clubbed to death—never tortured, but killed with brutal violence as those murdered Apaches had been. And each and every body was found scalped. The village of San Felipe was almost depopulated, while the villagers made their plans and laid their traps for the marauder. They might as well have tried to trap a ghost. Finally, in desperation, they packed up one and all and quit the village. Nobody remained in San Felipe unless it was the ghosts."

Vetch frowned, again remembering. Mexico was an ancient land, steeped in legend and superstition, saturated with the dark hybrid ways of cultures old and new. Vaguely he recalled a tale he had heard many years ago, of a so-called "Ghost of San Felipe," a malign and bloodthirsty spirit that came in the night and killed until it had choked off the life of a town.

Vetch thought, *Maybe he's not far from it at that*, and felt a distinct chill rack his spine. Angrily he shook himself. This was no time to spook; the enemy was flesh and blood—an enemy, moreover, whom he could now understand a shade better.

"Sam," Sara murmured. She leaned toward him in her intensity. "Don't be mad again—but listen. He is not human—not, I mean, as you are, or any man you've ever met. It would be no disgrace to refuse to fight him; only a fool would think the less of you. Why stay here and throw away your life—for nothing?"

"That matters to you."

"It matters, Sam. Very much."

"And Jimmie Joe?"

"What do you mean?"

Vetch shook his head. "I can't rightly say— not for sure. Maybe, however I want to put it, it boils down to a streak of damn-fool cussedness on my part. I don't cotton to a notion of any man alive being able to tell me where or how I can live. In effect that is what it would come to if I let him push me off my land. Making a stand here, cut off from most everything like we are, is like handing him all the odds. But there's worse things than dying, Sara. Leastways for a man there are. Do you understand that?"

"I think so. Sam, if that were all, I would face with you—whatever came. But I swear I'll die before I let him take my boy; that is what I care about."

"I never reckoned you were afraid for yourself," Vetch told her. "But suppose I sent you away from here with the boy, so far away even he could never find you. Even so, you wouldn't have Jimmie Joe. You might think you had saved him from something, but you still

wouldn't have him—in the worst way possible.
We are fighting a lot more than one Apache; we
are fighting for the heart of that boy. That
means that he has got to be a part of it, Sara,
and be involved himself in what happens to us.
He has got to see it all with his own eyes and
know that what *he* thinks and what *he* does will
make a difference. He don't see that yet, and
maybe he never will. Or say he does, and still
chooses his own blood father. My way, at least
we will have a fighting chance with him. A hundred miles, a thousand miles away, it would
mean nothing. For all we could ever do that
would touch him, we might as well hand him
over to Salvaje now and be done with it."

From the yard came the dog's sudden, furious
barking, and Vetch stood and went to a window. Nick Tana was crossing the yard; he dismounted by the house and stepped to the
ground. Vetch came onto the porch, and Nick
nodded greeting. "You fetched a fine loud one,
Sam. He picked me up right off."

"He'll be needed," Vetch answered, and told
Nick what had occurred during his absence.
Nick lifted a foot to the veranda's bottom step,
thumbed his hat, and whistled softly, wryly.
"I'm a sucker," he said simply. "That's what he
wanted. There was plenty of track leading off
from the butchered cow, all right, but it petered
out on a solid stretch of granite outcrop. I
should have known; it was all too damn neat
and easy. But I had left Hilario on guard, and I
couldn't be sure the trail wasn't worth follow-

ing. It is damn lucky all he wanted was to talk with Miss Sara."

"This time," Vetch said grimly. "I don't have a notion of what's next or how it will come, but I don't aim to wait on him. Among other things he came here to kill me, Nick. He'll choose his own way in his own time, and it won't do to sit on my hands till he does. I mean to hunt him like I'd hunt a wolf that was pulling down my calves."

"Pity you can't poison-bait him like one." Nick slapped his reins against his palm. "Even if you crowd him, he will make you fight him on his terms, chief. When do we start?"

"First thing tomorrow. What we got on our side is numbers, four men to his one. Daytime there'll have to be a man on guard here at all times. He can keep watch in the bunkhouse and never be spotted, but he can pick up anybody who comes stealing in. Even if he's off his guard, the dog will give the alarm."

"And the rest of us'll hunt the hills," Nick nodded. "How about Cortinas and old Coombs? Will they be agreeable to lending a hand?"

"Hilario, sure, and I'm guessing Ned will too when I put it to him. He is too mean to let anybody spook him off."

When Ned Coombs rode in that evening after his ordinary day of work Vetch told him the whole story. After a predictable outburst of irascible griping that he wasn't paid to hunt varmints, the old man surlily agreed to join them. The four men held a council of war after supper, laying out the main lines of their strategy. To a question by Hilario, Vetch said there would be no need to post a guard at night; the dog would sound out a prowler and all they need do was keep their guns within reach. A day guard would be important because all but one man would be gone; by daylight too the guard could get a shot at the enemy if he were to show up.

That night, when Sara and the boy had already retired, Vetch went out to the tack shed with a dish of table scraps. The dog set up a wild barking at his approach in the dark, but subsided growling when Vetch spoke. Returning to the house, he went from room to room to make sure that the windows and doors were secure. Satisfied that all was well, he went to the parlor and extinguished the last lamp.

He stood for a moment in the darkness by a front window, studying the faint limning of outbuildings and the rugged lift of encircling hills against a cobalt sky; just topping the eastern crest was a thin sickle of new moon. *A right time for scavengers to prowl*, he thought; and was reminded of how the Indians stressed the passage of time by the ripening and waning moons, naming each according to the seasonal and personal meanings they evoked. For Salvaje, and himself as well, tonight might well mark the commencement of the stalking moon. For both were the hunters: it would be a savage game of stalk and counter-stalk, and neither would be hunting a passive prey. Nor did Vetch deceive himself that he would again catch the Apache off guard as he had today, only to let his chance slip away through a moment's fatal hesitation. Chance alone had allowed even that brief opening; there would be no others, and all the bitter regrets for a lost opportunity would change nothing.

He slept like a log, and woke casually when the first cold tincture of real dawn slatted through the cracks of the massive wooden shutters closed and barred across the window. Sara was already up; her side of the bed still bore the warm depression of her weight. He heard her stirring about in the kitchen; he smelled fresh coffee as he dressed.

He was yanking on his boots, stamping them tight on, when her scream cut through the house like a knife.

Within seconds he reached the kitchen, the question he had shaped dying on the first word. Sara stood backed against the wall; her face turning toward him was bloodless, and she lifted an arm and pointed at the back door. It stood open.

The body of the yellow dog had been spread-eagled across the doorway from the outside, its two right paws nailed to one side of the door frame, the left paws to the opposite side. And it had been neatly gutted. The raw red cavity where the belly had been was head high to a standing person. It was this, in bloody proximity, that Sara had found herself facing when she had opened the door.

Chapter Fourteen

Whatever fears she had entertained till now, it had taken this grisly sight finally to unnerve Sara Vetch. But she was a woman with iron in her and few if any illusions; within minutes after the single involuntary scream escaped her, she was again self-possessed. Her face was pale but her hands were steady as she poured coffee for her husband and Nick Tana while the two men knocked out the nails that supported the gutted carcass. The scream, faintly heard by Nick in the bunkhouse, had brought him on the run, pistol in hand, wearing only his pants hastily pulled over his underwear.

She had laid a fire and started breakfast, Sara had explained, and then, since the wood box was empty, had started outside to fetch more stove lengths. She had got no further than opening the door.

The nails had been driven, doubtless with neatly muffled taps, through the animal's paws and just deeply enough into the door casing to support the dead weight. The two men easily removed the nails and lowered the eviscerated body to the porch planks, then offered each other their speculations. Vetch's foremost concern was how in hell the dog's death could have been encompassed without a sound.

"He was likely killed from a little distance," Nick murmured. "But not too far off, dark as it was, and a gun would make a racket. I'd say an arrow."

Sara came to the doorway with their coffee. At Nick's questioning glance, she nodded. "Yes, he always carried bow and arrows for game. He would never hunt with the rifle—a matter of pride."

Nick sipped at his coffee, then turned over the dog's body with his bare foot. "There it is." Vetch saw the bloodstained hole in the animal's neck. "It wasn't almighty hard for him, Sam. He had to be somewheres up on the slopes while it was still light and seen the dog tied up down here. After it was dark and he was fair sure the mutt was asleep he stole down against the wind and got close enough to fetch it with the first arrow. Probably had the point smeared with any of a dozen herb concoctions that would kill right off."

So it seemed simple enough in retrospect, but

not all the implications of the act were. Still, several things besides the plain fact of Vetch's crassly underestimating an enemy were pointed up. From the heights above, Salvaje could easily study their every move when they were not inside. Any sparse patch of brush would offer him concealment while they never caught a glimpse of him. Also, what Vetch knew indicated that Salvaje's rifle and marksmanship were such that he could very likely kill or wing an exposed man from up there. It was a chilling thought, but really no more so than contemplation of the various steps the Apache could have taken after disposing of the dog. There was, for example, a quantity of coal oil in a can in the shed from which he must have filched the nails. He might have fired every building on the place with unhindered ease. That he hadn't chosen to do so was in its way the most unnerving aspect of the tableau.

Nailing the dead dog across the doorway was, taken by itself, only a cunning and harmless shock effect. The most it could do was unsettle someone's nerves. Yet unnerving the adversary was always a shrewd prelude to the real campaign, Vetch knew. *And the next move?*

There was a coldness in his belly; he brought himself from his mood with a brisk wrench, thinking, *One part of what he wants is clear enough, and that is to whittle you down. Let him do that and he has already won—and you're already dead, just as he said.*

While he and Nick and Ned Coombs were

saddling up after breakfast, Vetch warned them again. "We got only one thing over him and that is numbers. We are going to stay together all we can, but if it turns out we can't, no matter what we do, just see we don't lose track of each other." He paused pointedly. "If he wants to lay up a dreadful for one of us there ain't much we can do to forestall him. But one thing he's got to reckon with: numbers. He has a single-shot rifle, and if he gets one of us, he has to reckon with the fact that the other two stands a good chance of making cover before he reloads. Then, if they have his position spotted, they can take him from two directions. He can be depended on to keep that in mind, so see you do."

He led them up the south flanking slope, clinging where possible to the casual shelter of the scrubby timber here. If Salvaje were laid up not far distant, no need to give him a clear shot. If such were his intention, he had already had numberless opportunities, and the farther they rode from the place, the better his chances. Then too, from what Sara had said, he might base a course of action on nothing but pure whim, so how the hell could you anticipate him?

On a whim of his own, Vetch called a halt at the top of the slope. There were several particularly choice points where an enemy might elect to stake himself for a vigil. It might be a good idea to look them over. Rifle in hand, Vetch dismounted and clambered warily through the brush and rocks. Presently, as he sidled up to a massive outcrop just below the summit, he found the sharp pocks of disturbance in the soil that indicated that a man had squatted behind the outcrop for a long time. Now and then he had stirred to ease cramped haunches, leaving inevitable sign that a man might erase simply by smoothing the earth. But that artificial eradication could be detected by a trained eye. Salvaje, knowing that he had at least two excellent trackers to deal with, had disdained any effort to cover up. Squatting where the Apache had, Vetch took a neat view of his entire headquarters. *Likely he was sitting up here most of the night, and what sign there is shows he ain't an hour gone from here.*

Rising, Vetch worked around and out from the outcrop in concentric circles, scanning every inch of ground. He did not find the least sign to indicate the Apache's departure, and his cautious respect went up a notch. But this was stony soil; other kinds of earth would be less easy to negotiate without giving oneself away.

What concerned Vetch was that, by holding to difficult ground, Salvaje might make it impossible for them to take up or hold his trail for any length of time. But then came Nick Tana's sharp hail back off on the hilltop, and Vetch catfooted upward to him. Nick was on one knee beside a low fir, and he pointed out, first, the abrasion on the trunk bark where an animal had been tethered; next, what Vetch had already noted: the plentiful sign of a barefoot pony.

"Same as yesterday," Nick murmured. "Same pony. Another trick to lead us off like then?"

"Maybe," Vetch said. "But he had a reason for tying it here, Nick. He was watching the place last night; I found the sign down by that big outcrop. Let's try to follow this up, but go easy. Keep a sharp eye out."

The track cut straight back into heavy timber and followed a game trail that made a pine-flanked aisle winding into the shallow hills. Within a few minutes they were completely cut off from the ranch headquarters, but this time Vetch had no concern at being away. Hilario Cortinas would not be caught off his guard again. Should Salvaje repeat yesterday's tactic of leading astray so he could double back to the ranch, he would run into Hilario's rifle. His son was the lodestone that might tempt him to try, but almost certainly he would not thus repeat himself. A man like this lone Apache might regard all other men with a measure of studied contempt when weighing their capabilities against his own, but he had not kept alive this long, nor waged his private vendetta success-fully, by rash estimates of his enemies.

Vetch felt also, with a mounting conviction, that the influences that had misshaped Salvaje's life had chosen no mean material to warp. He was a clever and resourceful man by the stan-dards of any people or culture, and one could only conjecture what a mind like his, but less incredibly self-sufficient, might have achieved under more promising circumstances. One had only to remember how some years ago a single great man, Mangus Colorado, because of one act of white treachery and abuse, had led the Apache nation on a rampage of terror that had given statesmen nightmares and made the best military strategists of the finest civilized army on earth look like fumbling children.

Here in the high pines, as the trail steadily climbed, the bracing thin air retained a morning chill; the labored breath of men and horses streamed away on a fine breeze, and the riders huddled into their mackinaws. Old Ned Coombs hunched deeply over his pommel, grimacing. Vetch ranged back beside him and asked what was the trouble.

"It's my goddamn humors again," the old man grumbled. "All your doing. There ain't nothing settles my humors but Dr. Fahnestock's Celebrated Vermifuge. You didn't fetch me no Peter's Pills either."

Vetch, at the time, looked away to cover a grin; but they had not gone far before the matter ceased to be a laughing one. There was no sham to the old man's pain, and after a spell of watching him grab his belly Vetch told him to get back to the place. "Ask Sara to give you some paregoric, then stay in your bunk."

"I don't need no paregoric! It's my humors acting up."

As old Ned rode slowly out of sight on the back trail, Nick, who was scouting trail a little ahead, fell back by Vetch's stirrup. "Is he really sick like he says, or does he put on?"

"Neither one nor the other," Vetch grunted. "He builds up a little ache in his head till it is something fatal, but he believes it right enough. Last spring he got swiped in the belly by a log we was using to prize up a lopsided shed onto blocks, and I think it bruised his innards. Hate to take chances with a man his age, so I give him his way."

Nick gave the hard blue sky and spiked green fir tops a circling look, then lowered his glance. The twilight dimness of the forest held a dappling of sun seepage. "I don't like it, Sam. The sign is all too plain; he ain't made a try to cover up. If anything, he has made it damn' easy."

"I noticed that. Still I mean to keep after him; if we get on his tail once, we might run him down."

Nick said nothing; the skepticism lay in his eyes, and Vetch remembered what both Nick and Sara had said: that Salvaje would make him play the game on his terms.

Now Vetch fell into the lead and tracked, while Nick kept a lookout. Vetch wasted no hope of taking the Indian by surprise; that would be a rare coup even with a large band of ordinary Apaches. He did not attempt to crystallize any set plan, but if he and Nick could once locate Salvaje the two of them might be able to outflank and outfight him. They had worked this way before and always to good effect; on this Vetch staked his best hope of bringing the present enemy down.

They left the cramped turnings of the game

trail and emerged onto an open bench where the track continued clear as glass and string-straight across the grassy flats. Where the flats came to an end, falling off into a wooded valley, they found something else. The trampled and bloody grass at the edge of the drop-away indicated that Salvaje had killed his pony here. He had evidently cut its throat with a quick slash and the animal had broken away and plunged downslope. Already dead on its feet, it had dropped within a few yards. They found the dead carcass in a tangle of thorny brush; a quantity of meat had been hacked from a hind-quarter.

Nick said, "I'm surprised he kept his pony this long," as he squatted on his heels to inspect the dead animal.

Only an Apache would kill a horse for a few steaks when he had no further use for him, but why had Salvaje not killed him immediately on reaching his destination, since, Apache-like, he would simply steal another when the need arose? Here the pony was not merely useless, but a burden, a large animal hard to conceal and easy to track. Perhaps he had kept the beast alive this long merely to lead them on another false scent.

Nick said, "You want to scour about here a ways? I'm guessing that even if we locate any sign, it will be the devil of a time following him afoot. And he can easy go where our horses can't."

"No. We'll head back to the outfit, Nick. I feel

way-down hollow about this, and I ain't sure why. Hilario is watching the place. But that 'Pache had something in mind leading us this far—either a piece of bad work, or he is trying to nerve us up more. I won't take a chance."

"I could try to take up his trail while you ride back."

Vetch shook his head. "No, he might want that too—to split us apart. I'm gambling he would have a hell of a time taking us both on, and he might be figuring that. We better stick together, Nick, always."

They retraced at a brisk clip the ground they had covered since early morning, not failing to keep their eyes open for almost anything. The real hell of dealing with an enemy who would not show himself was trying to anticipate him by guess and b'God, knowing that any of a dozen unchosen alternatives might be the best course. True in spades when you were up against one like Salvaje.

As well as filling his belly by killing his pony, the Apache had given himself a permanent advantage. Afoot, his wily woodcraft would make it next to impossible to pick up his trail if he chose otherwise. Nor, in this irregular, heavily timbered country, did he lose anything tactically by being rid of his mount; it would be different on flat and open country. Yet even there a horse's speed for a limited distance was, for an Apache, his sole advantage. For an Apache warrior would ride his horse to death in a short time, and then, equipped with only a little rancid water in a crude bottle fashioned of horse gut, carry on at a tireless jog trot for incredible lengths of time. He might cover a greater distance in a day than a horsebacker at a conservative pace.

The slaughtered pony had been killed not over an hour ago—plenty of time for Salvaje to achieve a wide lead doubling back, if that were his intention. And so Vetch hurried.

They passed the place on the trail where Ned Coombs had parted from them earlier, and a little farther on they found the old man's horse. Its carcass lay across the trail, and even before he had swung to the ground, Vetch could see that its throat had been neatly cut, exactly like the Apache pony's.

Nick slipped his rifle from its scabbard before stepping away from his mount, and he said in a whisper, "The old man?"

"No telling." Vetch had lowered his own voice. "We'll get off the trail and go ahead on foot a ways." He made a spare gesture that sent Nick, noiseless as a snake, into the undergrowth crowding the west side of the trail. Vetch slipped behind a screen of thickets on the opposite flank and glided along low-crouched, parallel to the narrow ribbon of trail that he barely kept in sight through the foliage.

Then a deep-angled crook of the trail brought him suddenly into sight of Ned Coombs. Vetch froze silently to a stop and balled himself down tighter in his leafy cover. A man who let himself be surprised into sudden moves was a man selling short his survival. Nick had been trained in the same harsh school. Across the trail he would also be halted and watching.

Before them was a sight that would shatter the control of toughened men only a shade less disciplined. The old man's body was hung by one foot from a branch ten feet above the ground, suspended by his own rope. His inert weight revolved in an idle clockwise turn. His free leg, projecting and bent at a stiff angle, pulled his dangling body awry and lent it a grotesque shape. The body was recognizable as old Ned's from the dissicated frame and the clothing. There was no other way, for it had been cleanly beheaded.

At last Vetch found a full answer to the half enigma of Salvaje's method. True, he had certain goals; he was also waging a war of nerves. But these matters were suddenly incidental to the separate sequences in his grim game. First the dog, and now Ned. Salvaje was amusing himself. He was playing with them as a cat would play with a nest of mice—while he calmly killed them off, one by one.

Chapter Fifteen

To spare Sara the sight of old Coombs's mutilated corpse, Vetch swung behind the barn as soon as he and Nick rode off the last slope above headquarters, rather than riding past the house to the corral. The two of them now reined through the big double doors into the musty barn, there dismounted and untied the decapitated body lashed to Nick's horse.

Vetch felt the heavy hand of blame. Salvaje must have lured them on, hoping to catch one of them alone to inflict an atrocity. And Vetch, who had foreseen the danger of his men's splitting off singly, had let just that happen. Instead of blaming old Coombs's ill-timed bellyache, he berated himself for letting the man ride back alone.

As they covered the body with a piece of tarp

Hilario, having seen them ride in, came from the bunkhouse and joined them. He listened impassively, then shook his head. "I did not like the old one, but I am sorry for this. It is a dirty way for a man to die."

"That was the idea," Nick observed. "War is a dirty business and you see governments giving it a clean look by passing out medals, playing up heroic doings, allowing honorable treatment of prisoners, and what not. A man who sees war as dirty as it is and fights it that way rakes in the pot every time."

Hilario shook his head again. "Maybe the good way to fight him is with many men. There must be many in maybe fifty miles around who would come here with their guns and help us hunt for the Apach'. A thing like this is everybody's fight."

Vetch disagreed. "If a lot of men came beating the hills he would only need to lay low till they gave up. Time don't count for anything in his way of reckoning. Or he could pick them off at his own pleasure while they never got a sight of him. Before you knew it they would be shooting at everything that moved, not ruling out each other. No. Two men who know their business have the best chance of running him to ground. From now on, Nick and me will be hunting on foot. We'll stay off the beaten trails."

"Good sense." Nick nodded. "That's how he'll play it from here on, now he has killed his horse. A man on horseback makes too easy a target, and a horse is a damned nuisance when you're tracking in country like this. If we stay off the trails he can't lay up fer us and he'll find it a sight harder to know our moves. Another thing, Sam. If he comes by night again, we best try to have something set up for him."

"I been thinking on that too." Vetch thumbed his hat off his sweaty brow. "It turns dark early these days, and there are maybe nine hours before it is light enough to make things out. Say we split up that time into three watches. That'll allow each man six hours' sleep, which is a sufficiency."

"At night," Hilario protested, "what can a man see? What can keep this damned Apach' from coming down off the hills and getting ver' close?"

"Nothing," Vetch admitted. "But once he *is* close, a man on watch might pick him up, depending on how much moon or starlight there is. You boys will have the best vantage point from the bunkhouse, and I'll have to handle my shift from the parlor window. I could come to the bunkhouse, but if he was watching from up above and spotted something out of the way it would spill the beans. It's important that he don't know there's anyone on watch; then he might walk into one of our guns. He can always guess, but a guess maybe won't keep him back."

"You alone cannot watch every part of your big house, señor. If he should come in the night and one does not see him, it could be ver' bad."

"What worries me," Vetch said, "is fire. If all the windows and doors are locked he can't get in without making a noise of sorts. But a fire could get started and be out of control before a man knew anything. All we can do is make it hard for him. There are three five-gallon cans of coal oil in the shed yonder. I want 'em moved to the storeroom in the bunkhouse and a padlock put on the outside door."

When this was accomplished Vetch felt eased on the score of fire. The thick logs of the house would take flame with difficulty, yet if a fire once got started it might quickly rage out of control. This remained a cogent fear, therefore: not merely the vulnerability of his house but the possibility of its destruction. All that he had here, land and family and home, were inseparably linked in his mind. He had selected with painstaking care every stick and stone that had gone into the building of this house; it was the stage and center of whatever his life had come to mean. Whenever he considered the matter, thought of danger to his house caused him, quite literally, deeper concern than his own possible death.

That evening he broke the news of Ned's death to Sara. He was reluctant to state the details; she pierced his evasive manner at once. "Sam, there is more to this." He told her the rest, and discovered a new composure in her manner.

And later she told him, "I don't know. Perhaps it's only coming to realize fully what a good thing we've found here. It took me time to learn what the feeling really meant. Of course I'm afraid. But fear—anything—is tolerable when you have a thing to believe in, a thing worth saving and defending, even worth dying for. Now—" Her eyes were alight with a force and a pride that showed more than any words the substance of her meaning. "Now if you were to tell me that you were sending me and the boy away till this was over, I wouldn't let you. If you told me that it was your true wish, I wouldn't let you. You could tell me, Sam, but I wouldn't believe it."

Vetch took the first guard shift that night, and when three hours had elapsed, watched the darkened bunkhouse until he saw a match flare briefly behind a window. That was Nick's signal, meaning that Nick was taking up the watch and now Vetch could safely retire.

He slept out his six hours soundly, and at dawn made a check of the house and yard, finding that to all appearances nothing had occurred in the night. Then Nick Tana approached from the bunkhouse and quietly disabused him of the notion.

"He was down around the place, all right," Nick said, low-voiced. "I checked the old man's body. When I lifted the tarp the head was there. He came in the night and left it."

Another act in Salvaje's quiet, ghastly war of nerves. It was a calculated and deadly thing, this deliberate outraging of the very roots of an enemy's being, his sense of decency. A man's culture imbued him with a very specific set of eternal verities that were supposed to survive hell or high water; he felt angry and naked and helpless when an outsider quietly and ruthlessly, by word or act, proceeded to demolish his various postures. It was a bit like watching a piece of the universe crumble to pieces, so explicitly were men fixed in the delusion that their attitudes where damned near everything was concerned had something to do with reality.

It would take a man like Salvaje, who believed in nothing at all, fully and unerringly to exploit such a fact of his enemy's nature. The white-eyes were foolishly squeamish because they had learned to be: that was what civilized decency finally amounted to, and Salvaje knew it while he bent it to his own use. *I can read him*, Vetch thought, and was made vaguely uneasy by his own understanding.

The worst of this form of mental attack was your near-total lack of defense. You could read him for all you were worth; you could brace yourself for new outrages and still, because the bald barbarisms offended sensibilities shaped outside your usual controls, you felt the jungle crowding in. You were chilled and revolted, and each separate atrocity crumbled another infinitesimal fragment of your world and left you a bit more naked than before.

Simply thinking on that settled Vetch on burying Ned Coombs in the yard in full sight of the house and bunkhouse. That would preclude the very likely possibility of Salvaje's exhuming the body for further unpleasant uses;

even at night he could not trouble this grave without being discovered.

With that done, again leaving Hilario on guard, Vetch and Nick prepared to take up the enemy's trail afoot. They went over the trampled barn lot that Salvaje had crossed the night before, and ferreted out enough faint track to determine his line of departure. They followed it past the outbuildings, and found easy going for a time. Once more the Apache had not attempted to disguise his tracks; there was a flaunting mockery in the trail of broken twigs and heel-pocked loam that rambled upslope. Then the sign began perceptibly to fade, and by the time they reached the crown of the rise it was, for all purposes, virtually invisible. They picked up enough here and there to fix the Apache's direction, but since he repeatedly made broad zigzags a few yards of straight tracking was the limit. Always they had to follow a fresh-angling spoor with the result that, by the end of a hot, bitter hour, they had covered less than fifty yards.

"Let's throw it up, Sam," Nick said in disgust. "He could already be thirty miles away and he ain't half trying; he is only playing with us now."

They sat down to smoke and rest and reshape their plans. The conversation was low-pitched and curt, for both felt keenly the humiliation of this. Had he been asked, Vetch would have sworn that no man alive could defy the tracker's perceptions that he had honed to acuteness over fifteen professional years. Nick's ability coupled to his added swiftness to sureness. Now they were up against a woodcraft so uncanny that it verged on the superhuman. Their quarry could lead them up a thousand blind alleys for the hell of it. Vetch was feeling more and more like a fly involved in a futile struggle with a sticky web.

They decided to switch to a blind search that would be as systematic as possible. They would square off small areas in their heads and agree on natural landmarks to represent the corners. Keeping a judicious distance apart but within easy contact by both voice and sight, they would cover each square thoroughly. Considering the nature of their enemy, the procedure seemed near hopeless, but outside of a passive waiting, they had no choice.

For the rest of that day and for many days to follow they doggedly hiked hill and flat, timber and meadow, working out in every direction from headquarters. Again and again they rechecked old ground. Salvaje chose to be coy. He left fresh scattered signs here and there to let them know he was not neglecting them, meanwhile abandoning direct action in his war of nerves. Apparently he wanted to keep them on edge but judged that a taste of his method would suffice; the anticipated unknowable provided as effective a nervous erosion as anything, and like any Indian male Salvaje evidently exerted himself toward nothing that resembled unnecessary work. That was for women. He kept them aware that he was in the vicinity, and this was enough.

Through each long night they and Hilario kept up a three-shift duty. Vetch's main hope now was that Salvaje might be emboldened to take some new nightly action. As the moon waxed toward full, Vetch cautioned Nick and Hilario to double their vigil; during those few nights that the moon stood at bright fullness they would stand the best chance of detecting a prowler.

Yet no matter how a man maintained the defenses of his alertness, even steady tension took on a monotony that was oddly soporific: in back of a good vigilance you nodded. Salvaje, knowing, might make the most of it at some time of his choosing.

Vetch was on the same game trail where a few days ago he and Nick had tracked Salvaje's pony when a shot came, whistling past his head and hammering into a pine bole, followed by the deep boom of a Sharps. In an instant Vetch had ducked off the trail into the dense trees. He made a quick contact with Nick, signaling him to close in on a thicket located at a slight distance. They inched onto it from different sides and with extreme care. A careful reconnoitering, then a search of the thicket, showed nothing but a small tunnel cut neatly through the foliage, twigs and leaves having been stripped away. Here Salvaje had waited to get a target. Vetch squatted in the big prints and sighted down the clean avenue of the shot that had missed his head by perhaps two inches. He had a wicked taste of the significance of this. The sudden silence after a lengthy lull had left a pulsing tension with him.

But Salvaje had calculated more, and wanted Vetch to know it. From here the trail was entirely visible at the point where Vetch was when the shot had come, and at this distance the miss could only have been deliberate. *He wants to be sure that I know he can kill me any time.* But Vetch had been careless too, following that trail. Nick severely observed as much. Salvaje could not otherwise have anticipated him enough to set up this mock deadfall. Since the Apache had vanished like a wraith within seconds after firing and the afternoon was growing late they quit for the day.

Tonight Vetch was again on first watch, but the lonely vigil was heightened by an oddly expectant quality. He did not believe in second sight, and he supposed that he was affected by today's excitement. Or perhaps it was the still, spectral beauty of the night. The sky was frosted by a white dusting of stars; the moon made a midday brightness where it touched, and the edges where it met black shadow gave an amazing detail to individual objects.

Even as he idly reflected how anything that moved would stand out in bold instant pattern, movement came. His gaze shuttled to focus as the shape of a man broke away from the large shadow of an outbuilding. Not really running, yet moving with a smooth, bounding swiftness, the figure crossed the open yard to a second shed cut off from Vetch's view.

Vetch wore his Colt in its holster; a rifle leaned against the wall close by his elbow. A long-barreled shotgun lay across his knees. He had started to bring up the shotgun, but he abandoned impulse; he could never have drawn a bead in the fraction of time that the prowler had entered and vacated his line of vision. If he had, the man's quickness and the elusive play of moonlight would have baffled his aim. But quick or not, he had recognized the giant form of Salvaje.

Heart pounding, Vetch crouched in the dark parlor on the edge of his chair. He continued to watch the yard, but with a bare attention; now he was listening rather than looking. The way that the stalker was skirting the yard showed his intention of approaching the house, but from which side? Unable to tell, Vetch ached to catch any alien noise.

Long minutes trickled by. His mind was not exaggerating the time that passed; he had placed his watch on the windowsill where a shaft of moonlight touched. *Fifteen minutes, now* . . .

A floorboard creaked lightly.

He stiffened, turning his head very slowly toward the black oblong of the corridor that connected the parlor with the bedrooms branching off it. The sound was one that a man lying awake at night, listening to his quiet house, ordinarily would notice barely or not at all. Even on this kind of watch, the sound would usually excite no more than a passing thought. The house was new and the boards not yet settled; vagrant noises were commonplace. But tonight, knowing that his enemy was close, Vetch would have weighed even a sound that he was not sure he hadn't imagined.

And he had not imagined that distinct and isolated creak, caused, he was ready to swear, by a man taking a stealthy pace and next putting his weight on that foot preparatory to a second step. The shift in the balance of weight had squeaked a board; the sudden break off in the sound indicated that the man had frozen in place. That was a mistake, for had he eased up his weight slowly, the creaking would have ebbed in a natural way. Salvaje was not familiar with floors.

Knowledge of a dangerous presence standing immobile not six yards away made a bewildering clash with his clammy certainty that Salvaje could not have got inside—not in complete silence. Each door and window had been checked carefully. *Then how?* Since the Apache was in the bedroom corridor that opened only onto the parlor he must have entered by one of the bedroom windows. Each window was covered by wooden shutters that, being located inside the sashes, could be unbolted only from the inside.

With that thought came the answer, jolting Vetch. If Salvaje could gain Jimmie Joe's attention, perhaps by a light tap on the glass outside, the boy could then admit him—and explain the trap waiting for him . . .

Whatever deviltry the Apache had had in mind in coming tonight and effecting a silent entrance, he had no doubt somewhat revised his plans on learning that Vetch was waiting for him in the parlor. Then, unable to resist some personally satisfying gesture that the situation would provide, he had stealthily eased open the door of Jimmie Joe's room. Only an unstable board had given him away.

The corridor doorway was almost opposite the window by which Vetch sat. He was not framed against the moonlight, but seated well to the side within the heavy shadow banked along the wall. Here he was on a line with the corridor. Could Salvaje make him out? Even if he could see better in the dark than most men, the Apache could surely perceive no more than dim shapes against this solid blackness. Vetch, straining his eyes into the mouth of the dark corridor, could make out absolutely nothing. Other than turning his head when the board creaked, he had remained unmoving. But he was about ready to move, his action already formulated.

The hallway was fairly wide, and he could not place the exact location of the groaning board. But it would sound again when relieved of the weight pressing along it, and then he would have his target. He would move only when Salvaje did.

Salvaje moved. Vetch half dived from his

chair, melting to the floor. In that instant the Sharps made its thunder, deafening between the narrow walls. Simultaneously Vetch squirmed his elbows along the floor to bring the shotgun into up-angling aim. The gun flash washed into his eyes and he was momentarily blind; but he had his aim. He pulled one trigger a moment after the rifle slug smashed into the wall above his vacated chair.

The blast of the heavy Greener shattered the confined echoes of the Sharps. A chaotic moment later he heard a door wrenched open; he let go with the second barrel, his aim altogether blind this time. On the heels of the gun roar Vetch heard something in one of the bedrooms crash to the floor. Scrambling to his feet, he threw the shotgun aside and palmed up his pistol as he lunged down the hallway. At its end he saw Jimmie Joe's door hanging open, and wheeled into the room.

Moonlight streamed through the window whose shutters were wide, the sash flung up. Vetch stood listening in the near dark. He heard only the whispery sigh of the boy's breathing from the bed. He fumbled for the lamp on the dresser and, shifting the gun to his left hand, wiped a match alight and touched it to the wick. From behind him, as the sickly flare of light grew, came a little stir of sound that yanked him around, hollow-bellied.

Sara stood there in the doorway, barefoot, one hand pressed to the ruffles at the bosom of her nightgown. She held a heavy revolver, and now lowered the weapon to her side. Vetch eyed the boy, who sat upright in the blankets and hugged his knees. His eyes blazed black defiance.

"He let him in, Sara."

"Yes," she said wearily, and let her eyes briefly close as she leaned a shoulder against the door jamb. "In the hall, Sam. When I came down the hall I touched something—I think you hit him."

Vetch grazed past her into the corridor; he held the lamp low to the floor. There was blood on the planking, and now, holding the light higher, he saw that a wet darkness spattered the wall hip high to where Salvaje had been standing when the first buckshot charge had cut loose. The hot fine wire of exultance burning in his belly died with thoughts of sober immediacy.

Moving back to Jimmie Joe's room now, Vetch found that the door had taken the full freckling of the second blast, perhaps an instant after Salvaje had wrenched it open and gone through. He saw a bright stippling of blood drops running over the floor and across the windowsill. Crossing the room, Salvaje had knocked over a chair, the crash Vetch had heard. Though he had left a fair amount of his blood behind, from his quick rally and escape he must have taken only a flesh wound. He was probably far gone by now. Still Vetch decided on a search of every building on the place.

Now both Nick Tana and Hilario Cortinas came bursting in without ceremony, brought by the shots. Vetch used few words in telling what had happened and then, armed with lanterns and ready pistols, the three of them made a building-by-building search of the whole headquarters. They found no Apache, but for once there was plentiful sign that hadn't been left deliberately. He had been badly limping in his escape. The dark spots of his blood pocked the dun earth under the pooling lantern as they followed the tracks between two outbuildings. They ended where the near-bare earth gave way to a mottling of light brush climbing onto the timbered slope beyond.

Vetch said, "We can't follow him in that timber by night. I don't reckon he'll get too far. Even if he can keep going, these tracks say he can't go fast."

They went back to the house and, in a certain atmosphere of mild exulting, examined the stained logs and floor in the bedroom corridor. Nick pointed to the big stain on the wall logs. "He won't be sitting a spell, and it'll hurt like hell to hunker. You nailed him in the right thigh and buttock as he was turning, Sam. His limp says the same thing. A good night's work."

"No," Vetch said meagerly. "He's alive."

"Man, nobody has come this close to amending that."

"He's alive," Vetch said again. "Get your sleep. We'll be going after him first light."

Chapter Sixteen

Feeling that the end of the bitter stalking was near, Vetch got little enough sleep himself. The first thin relief of false dawn brought him out of a restless doze. He dressed and made his breakfast, and then sat at the table by lamplight to dismantle his pistol, oiling and cleaning the parts. There was no need for this, but anything to fetter his impatience till there was light enough to track by.

While he was carefully reassembling the weapon Sara came to the doorway, fully dressed. She had not slept for staying up with Jimmie Joe after last night's violence, and circling shadows lay beneath her eyes. He had long ago noticed how the irises of her fine eyes seemed to expand and darken during moods of worry or concern; in this bad light they had a black oneness with the pupils.

"You're going now?"

"When it's light enough." He nodded vaguely toward the east wing. "He asleep?"

"Yes—at last. He pretended to be for a long time. He knows his father—I mean Salvaje—"

"That's all right," Vetch murmured, the acrid bitterness coming in full flood tide as he had not felt it. "He's *the* father, all right. There'll never be another. I was a fool."

She crossed quickly to his side; her hand lay gentle on his shoulder. "Sam—Sam." That was all; she had no false assurances for him, and this honesty of hers had taken his fancy from the first. At last she added, "He knows you wounded Salvaje; he will probably try to run away now and find him the first chance." Her voice broke. "Sam, I don't know what to do—whether perhaps I shouldn't let him."

Vetch looked up quickly, and the naked despair in her face shocked him. He reached for her hand, saying, "No. I didn't mean what I said." He hesitated. "I reckon I feel that way right enough, that it is damned near hopeless with the boy. But not all, not yet. If I did think so I couldn't make myself stop trying, Sara. Neither can you."

He glanced at the window, then came to his feet. The light was growing, and it would presently be time. He went to the door and reached his hat off a peg, feeling the darkness of her gaze. Soberly he said, "You lock Jimmie Joe in his room. I'm going to nail a couple boards over his window so he can't get out that way."

"How long can we keep him locked up?"

"Until this is over, anyhow. I mean till I have his pa, one way or the other." His eyes squinted half shut. "I don't know. As long as there's the boy—maybe I should take him alive. Try, anyway."

"No!" The one vehement word burst from her before he had finished. "Don't try, Sam! Don't take a single unnecessary chance with him! The first time you're aware of him, even if you're not sure, shoot to kill." She put out a hand blindly, her words dipping to a whisper as she came swiftly to him. "Bring yourself back alive—that's all I care about."

The clean darkness of her long hair, loose around her face, was a silk-fine crumple under his palms flat against the inward curve of her strong back. He tasted her lips, full and giving.

He went out into the morning; he scared up two pieces of sawed lumber and nailed them crosswise over the boy's window. Afterward he fetched his rifle and went to the bunkhouse, where he found Nick ready to go. The half-breed had stayed up on his usual dogwatch guard, and now Hilario took over.

Vetch was taking no chances; before he and Nick departed he gave Hilario a special word of caution. They didn't know how badly Salvaje was really injured. He might have put a good distance between himself and here in order to lie up and tend his wounds. Or he might circle back here at an early time. For now, hurt and murderous with the odds suddenly turned against him, he would surely abandon his deadly game of cat and mouse. He would delay no longer but would gamble all on an attempt to spirit his son away.

Sara came out to the porch and watched as he and Nick crossed the yard from where Salvaje's flight had carried him into the timber. She and Vetch had said their good-bye, and he only turned and raised his hand as they reached the trees; she lifted hers in reply and quickly turned back into the house.

The two men angled up through the timber to the summit of the hill. The trail was glaringly plain: a route of snapped twigs, bruised bark, and fragmented bits of loam. Even a greenhorn could not have missed the dried dark spots that showered the way.

They crested the hill and came off its far side, following an easy track into the ridges beyond. Here the land lapped up into great corrugated folds, a succession of corduroy rises that bristled with spiky black timber. Fat milky caterpillars of ground mist filled the swales between them. The early sun broke in prismatic gem lights on swatches of dew-washed meadow; the cold air was wine-like to taste.

Timber and grass yielded to rougher going as the ridges became seamed with ravines and broken-surfaced with craggy spurs and loose boulders. Instinctively Salvaje had headed for the nearest terrain where pursuit would be hardest; he had not given way to panic, for the sign showed him forging slowly and deliberately, never hurrying, toward the southwest. But he could not cover a limp severe enough to make him slightly drag his foot on his hurt side. Now and then his trail cut away at deep angles, a systematic meandering over select patches where tracking would prove most difficult.

They pressed steadily forward, toiling up and down endless steep ridge faces. Always they kept watchful, rarely communicating except to alternate their concentration; one man was constantly on the lookout while the other tracked.

They sweated and grew hot, though the climbing sun had a misty and colorless appearance that occasioned Vetch some deep uneasiness. The heavy and unstirring air presaged rain; a storm would cancel his hopes simply by wiping out the trail. He only hoped that it would hold off awhile longer. He had a tingling sense that they were nearly onto their man.

He panted, as they toiled up a stony ridge flank, "He might lay up if he thought he lost us. But he is leaving enough sign for a bull buffalo, and he sure as hell knows it."

Nick nodded. "Best he can hope for is to make things hard as possible and slow us, which he is. Maybe, though, he's only trying to gain enough time to let him stop a spell. If you or me was hit like him, we would have gone down long before this. Any man would of but him."

"Wonder if I didn't hit a tendon. He is favoring that leg plenty."

"Well, for sure you mangled it to hell. He is losing too much blood, and he'll pump out a lot more while he stays moving. Not to say all that shot in his rump ain't a mean load of pain to tote on the run. He can't but want a break to dig it out before too long."

They came onto the crest of this tall ridge and took a breather. It was the last of the corrugated formations, and ahead was a squat flat-topped promontory whose long flanks were bare and flinty except for straggling lines of scrub timber. But its tabled crown was luxuriant with a grove of thick pines. Vetch and Nick exchanged glances with a common unspoken thought: that the place could not have been more ready-made for an ambusher if nature had so planned it. A man laid up with a rifle at the fringe of the high timber would have, as well as plentiful cover, a perfect view of the bald slope below that must be crossed to reach the top.

"If there's one thing wrong with it"—Nick broke silence dryly—"it's too damned obvious."

"But he's on his last legs, or close to it, and won't have much choice. I think he's there. Nick, this is the place to use the old plan. Just one thing. We'll be in the open nearly all the way till we reach the top, so both of us won't run at the same time. There's enough cover here and there to let a man run from one place to the next, say, at five-or ten-yard bursts. If he starts shooting, the man laid up will give the man running a cover fire."

"Running man will be wide open even so."

"We got repeaters and he can fire only once at a time," Vetch murmured. "He can't shoot at a man over once on each dash while the other can give him a heavy fire. I think the odds are with us, Nick. Or else we can wait down here and watch each side of the hill and starve him out."

Nick grinned and shook his head. "Nope. We don't even know he's up there, and this is the only way to make sure. Anyhow, I say crowd him. He is too damned snaky to be allowed a breathing space. Crowd him, Sam."

Vetch smiled and dropped a hand over Nick's shoulder. They discussed the approach briefly. They would fan out to left and right in separate arcs, parenthetically, and swing the arcs together at the point where their man was, catching him between in a pincers of gunfire.

They descended the last ridge, crossed a mountain rivulet that boiled through the divide, and breasted choking thickets as they started up the slow-mounting promontory. As the escarpment grew steeper and the brush began to thin away, Vetch gave Nick the nod; they split apart.

Vetch took the left tong of the pincers: he went upward at a noiseless moccasined lope, following the slope in an outward arc at perhaps a seventy-degree angle. He made his body as compact a target as possible, gliding through the fast-thinning brush. Always he watched the timber at the summit. His nerves twisted with the screw turn of tension. He had never felt anything this intense, and knew it was because of the personal stake involved.

He reached the last scraggly bushes; he dropped to his hunkers and turned his eyes toward the right where Nick would be. Nick was crouched behind a good-sized boulder; he flashed a grin and jerked his thumb upward, signaling Vetch to make the first dash.

Vetch clamped his hat on tight; he held his rifle out from his body as he sprinted up the bare slope. He had marked a tattered clump of bushes ten yards up as his first stop. He achieved it with sweat oozing from every pore, breathing through his mouth. Staring at the silent timber that was still well above him, he cursed under his breath. He looked back over his shoulder toward Nick Tana, then jerked a thumb upward. Nick ran with the lean bounding grace of an antelope; he came to another boulder on his arcing climb and dropped behind it.

My turn again. The air was heavy as cream, with a sluggish feel of cross drafts; it was too quiet. Vetch licked his dusty lips and blinked his stinging eyes. *Don't think about it; run*. He leaped up and ran hard and low and fast; he piled into a cluster of heaped rock fragments. He fell on his back and rolled over and scrambled on his hands and knees to the rock cluster. He hugged his cheek to the rock; it was cool for this time of day. The sky was clouding over. *It will have to rain soon. Suppose he's not up there? Maybe he went on and is a mile away. Don't think about that either. Go on, Nick—go on.* He brought up his thumb.

Again Nick ran. Nothing but the queer, padding rhythm of his moccasins broke the dead hush that brooded on the rocky scarp. Nick tumbled into the good shelter of a heavily gashed ravine; his hand appearing above its rim gave the signal.

The timber was much nearer now. *Why the hell don't he shoot? Don't think—run, run!* Vetch ran, and he came to a thrusting slab about five yards away and let his legs collapse, knowing how a scared buck felt. He burrowed against its flat-sided shelter, his breath hissing, and, barely exposing an eye, watched the timber. He would make the trees on the next dash, and sure as death Salvaje would shoot before then. If he were there.

Vetch's knees felt like water. He wanted to give the signal but he hesitated. If Salvaje were there, his reason for holding his fire was cold-clear: with his one-shot rifle he was under a handicap no matter how he met the attack. To betray his position by shooting at one man meant giving the other man a target for a raking fire. He had chosen, with an iron-willed patience, to let them almost reach the timber before he started shooting.

If he were there.

The trees were terrifyingly close. *I'll run,* Vetch thought suddenly. He would not give Nick the signal; assuming the brunt of the danger was his own duty.

And then the shot came, jerking his head around. Nick, not waiting for the signal, had started his dash, only to catch a hollow-nosed slug in mid-run. And in the head.

Vetch saw, even at this fair distance, the terrible, jaw-flapping impact. He could swear that he heard the slug hit. There was a strange separation of impressions as though time were telescoping outward, so that he was clearly aware of the shot's whole effect and still had time to let his gaze leap to the timber where sound still pounded and powder smoke shredded indifferently into the tired sunlight.

A drifting cloud cut off the misty sun rays. Without looking up, Vetch vaguely knew this from the drab fading of the tawny rocks. His eyes finished gauging the length of steep incline that remained between him and the first trees and, before the shot echoes receded, he was on his feet, legs pumping him in a last furious lunge. In him was the crawling knowledge that he hadn't enough time before Salvaje reloaded; this blind charge on an open slope was suicidal. But a wildness in him from what he had just seen would not let him hold back.

Yet for a straining moment, as he scrambled, panting, up a shallow bank to top a slab of shelving rock just below the trees, he thought he had made it. And in that same moment the slab tilted. The rotten granite split and crumbled, dissolving under his feet; he plunged downward in a rough, helpless sprawl. A shot, succeeded by the low bellow of the Sharps, whiplashed across his back as he fell: the fall saved his life. Loose earth and stone cascaded down with Vetch's body. Belly-flat to the bank, he taloned his fingers and dug in his toes, and broke his skidding fall. For a moment he lay half-stunned, bruised and bleeding; he still clutched his rifle. Then he was aware of a light thud of running feet.

Painfully he turned his head, seeing off to his right that Salvaje had left the trees and was sprinting down the hill in fluid strides. Even with his wounded leg held stiff, his spring-steel muscles bore him with the grace of a giant cat. He shot a fleeting glance at Vetch and bounded on without pausing. He must have broken from cover, thinking that he had hit Vetch—and no doubt would have stopped to finish him if he hadn't seen Vetch very alive and already swinging his Winchester to bear. Salvaje had blundered; encumbered by his empty Sharps and by a bad leg he plunged on downhill.

Vetch braced himself with his hip against the crumbling bank and, as fast as he could lever his rifle, raked the line of Salvaje's run with a fusillade of shots. Suddenly Salvaje went down in a brutal fall, dust moiling in churning clouds as he spilled head over heels, a savage momentum carrying him onward for a good five yards. Vetch's hoarse croak of exultance died when Salvaje lurched stumbling to his feet, covered with colorless dust. He swayed for a moment; he shook himself like a lion and looked wildly about him.

Vetch shoved away from the bank and came careening in a full-tilt run down the slope, pumping his magazine empty. A couple of near slugs screamed off the rocks close by, and Salvaje delayed no longer. His running fall had carried him almost to the pale green shield of shrubbery near the slope's base, and now he wheeled and melted away into it.

Vetch came to a dead stop, cursing under his breath; sweat cut muddy tracks down his dirt-smeared face. He scanned the brush for the fine tracery of movement that would betray the Apache's passage. No use: Salvaje had needed only that thin cloak of vegetation to cover his swift and silent escape.

Vetch forced his sore muscles into movement. He stumbled down the long stony escarpment to where Salvaje had fallen. No bullet had touched the Apache; his bad leg had simply folded in his wild run, and in the battering fall he had lost his rifle. He had briefly looked for the weapon, but was forced to abandon it with Vetch coming on the run, firing.

Vetch himself had to search for some seconds before he located the big gun. It lay flat and almost invisible against the incline, plowed into the floury dust, which had also settled over it. Vetch picked up the heavy rifle, hefting it. His eyes turning backward and up found the dark form sprawled on the rocks. An uncontrollable trembling gripped him. He dropped his rifle and fastened both fists around the Sharps, swinging it with a wordless savagery against a boulder. He brought it down again and again till the mechanism was smashed; the stock was fibrous splinters and the octagonal barrel was bent to an obtuse angle. He threw it aside and tramped back up the hill.

Nick lay bowed grotesquely on his belly across a rock as he had fallen, his head hanging down. Vetch knelt and raised his face and then, with a qualm of sickness, let his head settle back. There was nothing to do for Nick. His thoughts swung back to Salvaje with a new-dawning fear.

Even wounded and in a bad way, the wily Apache might have led them this far with intent. If so, his maneuver had partly succeeded. One of the two men trailing him was dead. He stood a good chance of beating the other back to the ranch where now only one man and a woman stood between him and his son. And now Salvaje was playing no games: he was a cunning and ruthless animal, hurt and dangerous, with a single goal set like a hot coal in his brain.

Chapter Seventeen

Vetch's whole body was one great ache from the fall he had taken when the granite slab collapsed. But driving urgency would not permit him even a few minutes of needed rest. He plunged into the brush where Salvaje had disappeared and retraced the trek across the choppy succession of ridges they had been most of the morning in crossing.

He told himself that Hilario Cortinas was on guard and that Salvaje would have to face Hilario's rifle. *His bow and arrows, though*, Vetch remembered. *But he wasn't toting them. Too bulky for this game. He has them cached somewhere.* However, if the cache were not close along a straight line to the ranch, Vetch guessed that Salvaje would not, in his condition, waste precious time and energy going off route to obtain them. That was cold comfort; even weaponless he was a formidable foe.

Vetch's hope was that the Apache's wounded limb would enable him to close the gap between them before Salvaje reached the ranch. The wound was pumping severely from this new round of exertion; his stumbling tracks showed that his splendid body was being steadily sapped of its vitality. He was drooping, and at one place he had plainly tripped and fallen.

Shortly the flinty bare ridges were behind him, and Vetch was on the grassy, timber-mantled slopes that characterized the terrain nearer his home. Now he slowed pace somewhat and tightened his grip on his rifle, watching the trees ahead. *I ought to be close onto him pretty quick.*

He was deep along a game trail that snaked over one timbered crest when he heard twigs crackle. Suddenly a lithe brown form broke from cover and dodged away through the trees. Vetch brought the Winchester to level and shot, thinking, *He was resting there*; and then the powder smudge cleared: Salvaje had vanished down the trail.

Spurred by knowing how close he was, Vetch broke into a full run. He charged through a brush clump that nearly overgrew the trail; his foot struck something. He heard a crack and a *whir* of something whiplike tearing the air; he caught a flash of steel. There was a slashing blow on his thigh, and then pain and blood.

He staggered back. A long razor-edged hunting knife had cut deep into the fleshy part of his thigh, and now with his movement the blade slipped free. Blood gushed and paralyzed him with the fear that an artery was severed. He dropped to his knees, seizing his leg almost groin high to bite off circulation.

He stared at the trap. It was like a child's snare, ingeniously simple, deadly, and unexpected. A low springy tree limb projecting across the trail had been slashed clean of twigs and leaves. The knife had been lashed crosswise near the end with a rawhide thong and the branch bent back in a deep horizontal arch. A dead bough, crotched at one end, had been placed at an angle to the ground so that the butt end was dug deep into the soft loam and the crotched tip held the limber branch back in its bent position. The slightest jar would have been sufficient to dislodge the delicate restraint. Vetch's foot tripping the primitive trigger had left the knife whip back in a semi-arc that ended at his thigh.

Probably Salvaje had hoped to find his abdomen, but had lacked time to spot a better-placed branch. This one had inflicted a cut that was a trifle low, but deep and effective. As well concealed as the trap was by screening brush, Vetch would certainly have noticed something amiss before he touched the trigger. Salvaje had rested up while waiting boldly to make himself the bait that would pull his enemy into a heedless run—and the trap.

Fat drops of rain began to fall. With his clasp

knife Vetch ripped his trousers for a better look at the wound. It was bleeding copiously but not pumping with his heart, he saw with relief. He tied it off with his bandanna, which was little help. He saw the rawhide thong securing the hunting knife to the sprung branch. He detached the thong with his knife and fastened it around his thigh for a tourniquet, using a stick to twist it for increased or lessened pressure. He was in a hurry, and this would have to do.

The rain came down a straight light drizzle. It was a strange storm; there was no wind, no thunder or lightning, only the dismal steady rattle of falling water on the trees. Vetch was soon soaked to the hide; he plodded on, pain and worry and a high tide of feverish impatience driving him. If the least that Salvaje had hoped for was to slow his pursuer, he had succeeded. The cut was deep and wanted to bleed; he had frequently to tighten the tourniquet, which caused his leg to stiffen and go numb, and he had to make as many stops to loosen the thong.

He hardly realized when he had topped the last crest above his home; the fever was becoming a reality. The dizziness and time lapses were only the opening symptoms, he knew, and thought, *Got to finish this soon—finish him*. He had halted, and now he removed his hat and pulled the sleeve of his wet mackinaw across his face. That harsh abrasion and the cold rain sluicing down his face cleared his head. He squinted down at the buildings. Billows of oily smoke were pouring from the stable doorway, fraying into the mizzling veil of rain.

A man came running out of the stable, swinging for the house. Salvaje. Vetch brought the rifle to his shoulder, trying to pull down on him through the rain; he blinked and cursed and let the barrel drop. It was too long a shot in this visibility, and his head was swimming. Where was Hilario; why had Salvaje fired the stable? There was no time to wonder. He had to get down there fast, and he hoped he had enough strength left to make it.

He went down the slope in long, heel-driving strides, disregarding the waves of pain that racked his thigh. By now Salvaje was no longer in sight. He had turned the corner of the house, and Vetch knew he was heading for Jimmie Joe's window. Sara must be inside the house, no doubt too preoccupied to have noticed the smoke; but Salvaje would have to break in to get Jimmie Joe, and that would seize her attention quickly enough. The cross of thick boards nailed across the window might defy his strength briefly, but he could tear it off barehanded. Vetch could only hope in his straining desperation that Sara would not try to stop the Apache.

As he reached the bottom of the hill back of the tack shed he was running in great painful lunges. He tried to cut his speed and veer off from the shed, but his awkward and stiffening leg and the greasy mud underfoot betrayed him. Fighting to break his momentum, he lost his slippery footing and plunged into the shed wall. By twisting his body at the last moment he saved his head; his shoulders and trunk caromed with slamming force against the heavy logs.

The next thing he knew was that he was sprawled on his belly by the wall; his nose and mouth were full of mud. Retching and spitting, he crawled groggily to his hands and knees. He braced a palm against the wall and lurched to his feet; a ragged pain knifed through his ribs. God—he must have broken a couple. He saw his rifle on the muddy ground and pawed it up; a vague plainsman's instinct, rather than any real presence of mind, made him peer in the muzzle for mud. He was still dazed; his ears sang with fever and slugging waves of pain.

Move, Goddamn you. Vetch forced his legs to leadenly stir, carrying him to the shed corner. Because it was difficult to walk, and since he was not even sure how many seconds he had lain stunned by the wall, he let instinct pull him to a halt; here was a full view of the house and the open yard. He teetered dizzily on his spraddled feet and dragged things into focus.

Suddenly Salvaje came into view from around the house; Jimmie Joe was slung across his shoulder like a sack of meal. Salvaje supported him with one hand; in the other swung a repeating rifle, and by this Vetch knew that Hilario Cortinas had also become the Apache's victim.

Let him be the last! Vetch hesitated in bringing up his rifle, hoping that Salvaje would veer back this way. He did not want to fire at this distance for fear of hitting the boy. Here he was almost concealed by the shed corner, and Salvaje might get quite near before spotting him. But the Apache did not swerve in this direction. As if by a kind of predetermined impulse he was quartering straight across the yard toward the southeast. Toward Sonora—his instinctive goal? Now he was running at right angles to Vetch's line of sight, presenting a fast target seen through a gray drizzle and a clogging weariness. Vetch's sights wavered on target; to shoot was to endanger the boy.

The yard was a lake of mud; some distance beyond the house Salvaje's foot skidded and he started to go down. Even wounded and burdened, with both hands occupied, he caught partial balance; he fell on one knee and swayed thus for a moment. Briefly it gave Vetch a stationary target, and he started to renew his sights. He did not aim to kill; he deliberately pulled the gun low to minimize risk to the boy. Then he was arrested by Sara's cry.

She had burst from the front door and was running off the porch toward the kneeling Apache, the heavy pistol Vetch had warned her to keep always near half lifted in her hand. Salvaje had started to spring up; her voice stopped him, and he turned his head. She cried out in Apache for him to put down the boy, and then, knowing that he would not do so, did not pause. She stopped and brought up the pistol, and shot at his legs or perhaps close to them; but the bullet gouged up a chocolate geyser of mud some distance away.

With a distinct growl Salvaje let the boy drop lightly to the ground, but not in obedience to her order. He wheeled on the instant, starting for Sara. Now she was directly in line with the Apache, and again Vetch's aim was baffled. She stood steady; she seemed calm, and she got the big Colt cocked—but then fired a shade too quickly.

Salvaje slightly broke stride; Vetch thought that his shoulder was hit. But he did not slow his long strides, and he flung aside Hilario's rifle. Before Sara could cock the pistol again he was on her, wrenching it from her hand and throwing it aside. He faced her for a moment; he shouted something and then struck her, a savage backhand blow. Sara started to fall, but he caught her and held her half upright, his free hand whipcracking back and forth across her face. He was smiling. He did not slap; he struck her steadily with smashing, openhanded blows.

Vetch let out a hoarse cry as he stumbled forward now, almost falling at each step. He wanted to draw Salvaje's attention, but the giant Apache's insensate rage appeared to block out everything else. Whatever object of spite or frustration Sara might represent, he was abusing her with a maniacal pleasure that each brutal blow built to a worse fury. A final blow knocked Sara to the ground, and, swinging his head, the Apache roared at his son—something about a knife.

The boy still stood where Salvaje had dropped him. His face was turned toward them, away from Vetch, who was obscurely glad of it. He did not want to see the savage distortion of Salvaje's example reflected there. Then the boy ran forward, yelling something, words that washed against Vetch's brain with a faraway roar like the distant surf of the ocean he had once seen at Matagorda Bay. Suddenly Salvaje bent and fisted a hand in Sara's hair and dragged her across the muddy yard toward the house.

Vetch, his legs grinding tiredly away, came to a fuddled stop. He felt a plodding amazement that he was no farther than he was. He was seeing things through a vast shimmer of distance, like a man in a dream. *No, this is real*, his mind insisted. *Shoot now, before he gets inside the house*.

He rasped a horny palm across his eyelids; now he could see. And what he saw, with a foggy surprise, was that Jimmie Joe was at his father's side and clawing at his father's arm, crying loudly. Finally Vetch caught the gist of the boy's words—*No, you must not cut off her nose*.

It was then that Salvaje, in the blind grip of his unthinking rage, brought up his free hand and cuffed his son solidly across the head. The force of the blow spun Jimmie Joe completely off his feet and knocked him rolling in the mud.

As Salvaje dragged Sara onto the porch Vetch was dimly aware of the boy scrambling to his feet, running this way a few yards and bending down. Vetch was straining to find his aim again when he realized that the boy had scooped up Sara's heavy revolver and turned it on his father; he was struggling with both thumbs to cock it. The shock of this momentarily touched Vetch and then, with an iron concentration, as the broad buck-skinned back floated into clarity, he took his half breath and squeezed the trigger.

Salvaje had nearly reached the door. The bullet taking him between the shoulder blades drove him with a crash into the heavy panel. He let go of Sara. The door yawned ajar with his leaning weight; his knees sagged. He slipped quietly onto his back on the wet planks.

Jimmie Joe stood motionless, holding the Colt pointed but uncocked; he had turned his head, startled, as Vetch had fired. He stood frozenly now as Vetch tramped up to him and lifted the gun from his hand.

"Let me tell you something, boy." Was that hollow wash of sound his own voice? "You are like to lose a hand that way, shooting off a gun plugged with wet clay."

Salvaje slowly turned his head as Vetch spoke, in time to see him taking the gun from Jimmie Joe. His gaze lighted on his son, and a smile flitted across his lips. *"Enju,"* Vetch heard him whisper. *It is well*.

Vetch went on to the porch; he stumbled and

fell to his knees by the step. He fumbled his way to Sara's limp form and found the strength to gather her in his arms. But he could not stand then. He sat there in a dull weakness and cradled her bruised, bleeding face in his hands; a residue of hate lifted his gaze to meet Salvaje's.

He saw, close up at last, a hawklike face quite as clean-chiseled and intelligent as the fine bronze profile on some rare medallion. The obsidian-black eyes kindled with little shifting lights, and now, wiped clean of anger, they were calm and mocking eyes. Somehow Vetch had known that they would habitually look exactly as they did. This gave him a strange sensation, sitting wounded and sick in the cold rain with Sara's wet weight across his knees.

But what else he saw in that lean-angled face was totally unexpected: a slow smile that bespoke his savage admiration as clearly as words might. He had found a worthy foe in the white man who had played out to the death his grim game. It was he who lay dying; he had never considered that, but still he smiled.

Again the smile turned to a satirical mockery. "You did not win, white-eyes," Salvaje whispered. "You did not—" The voice failed and sighed away, and the eyes became black glass. The smile remained.

In the moment that Salvaje had seen him take the gun from the boy Vetch had realized the Apache's belief that his son had seized the pistol to side with him against the white man. Having let him die mistakenly confident in that belief,

241

Vetch was often to wonder why. Nothing would have caused him less regret than destroying Salvaje as thoroughly as the Apache set out to destroy him.

A thread of understanding perhaps? He would never be sure.

Chapter Eighteen

As things turned out Hilario Cortinas was quite unhurt except for a new egg-sized bump on his head. He stood by Vetch's bed like a lean, muddy apparition, shifting about uneasily as he told how he had run out from the bunkhouse directly on seeing smoke curling out of the stable. Yes, a trap had occurred to him; but he was not certain that a horse or two was not stalled inside rather than being loose in the little fenced pasture off behind. Therefore he had hurried to investigate, and promptly as he entered the smoke-reeking stable he was hit without warning. But the blow was badly struck, and indeed laid him low for only a short while. Reviving, he found his rifle gone. Though choking and half blind with the smoke, he was able to locate a burning bundle of hay. It had been ignited, then made to smoke by wetting down; luckily the damp straw had not spread the flames to dryer stuff before he smothered the flames with his mackinaw. *Por Díos*, he had been greatly stupid for being caught twice in this way; he had no excuse.

But how had Salvaje reached the stable without being seen as he came off the slope?

Quién sabe? There was no way of telling; perhaps he, Hilario Cortinas, son of a stupid, had been careless. Or that Salvaje *diablo* had been sufficiently clever to descend the slope at the rear of the bunkhouse while Cortinas watched from the front. *Quién sabe?* The rain and the scatter of various outbuildings had lent the Apache sufficient cover to reach the back of the stable and enter unobserved.

Vetch merely grunted; he was thinking that quite likely Jimmie Joe had betrayed their whole strategy during his father's visit last night. That would be when Salvaje had learned of the daily bunkhouse watch.

Sara sat by the bed. She had changed to a clean dress, and appeared none the worse for the beating she had taken, except for her swollen and discolored face. She asked now, "Has the rain stopped?"

"Yes, señora."

"Then go to town and get the doctor. He must come soon, for Sam has been cut badly. There may be infection. One of his ribs is broken. Also I am afraid that he will take the grippe from being out with a fever in the rain."

The Stalking Moon

Hilario nodded his understanding and started to leave the room. Vetch said weakly, "Hilario, I want Nick Tana's body brought in as soon as you can manage it."

"Sí." Hilario hesitated. "The Apach', what about him?"

"Take him a good ways off in the hills." Vetch sighed as a slight shift of his body stabbed agony through his thigh, bulky with bandages under the quilt. He knew that the fever and the sickness were only beginning; he wanted to get these odd hang-fire details settled.

Hilario went out, his saucer-size rowels racketing through the house. Vetch looked hesitantly at Sara. "I want to bury Nick on the slope—by the baby?"

"Yes," she said softly. "I would like that, Sam." She tried to smile, but then grimaced painfully. "What a sight I must be."

She glanced toward the mirror above her little table, and started to rise from her chair as if to go to it. Vetch reached a hand and captured hers, and she sat back. He said quietly, "No need. You're beautiful."

"No. Not even—"

"Yes."

A tentative little smile brushed her lips; her head turned then toward the doorway. The boy stood there watching them. His face held a curious expression, a dumb-animal look that defied anything to pierce it.

Sara said crisply, "Jimmie Joe."

The boy straightened. His eyes were not quite

sullen, and he came slowly forward. "Jimmie Joe," his mother said very distinctly. "I want you to do something." He watched her with closed thoughts. "I want you to put your hand on his."

The boy did not move, and she said, "There— like this," taking his hand and laying it on Vetch's upturned palm. Then she took her hands away.

The boy stared down at his hand, brown and small against Vetch's big rawboned one that was weathered only a shade less dark than his own. Then he looked up.

Is it that important, boy? Vetch asked the question with his eyes only. *Maybe you know it isn't. You made that choice when you picked up the pistol, whether you know it yet or not. As an Apache would say, You are like a bat, being neither mouse nor bird. Not of one race or the other. You can go sour knowing that or you can take the best of two peoples, like Nick Tana did. He had a bitterness in him, but it never amounted to shucks beside the way he had of making them all know him as a man. In spite of it, and because of it too. Maybe you started to know that a little when you saw him beating her and remembered that you're of her blood too. And you found no shame in it when you thought of how through everything she had stood ready to die for you if she had to, as she was just then, Did you think of any of that, boy, and how much did it mean?*

He searched the boy's face for the old hatred; he saw the soft mask shred apart in a wild, mounting bewilderment. Suddenly the boy jerked his hand away, then turned and ran from the room.

Sara looked at her husband, despair in her face. "I thought that things might have changed a little. That the two of you—What's the use?"

"This much," Vetch said gently. "Do you remember how you were when we made our 'bargain'? How bad you wanted to be more than you were ready to be? But your trying made the start."

"Yes. But for him, Sam?"

"Well," Vetch said, and tiredly let his eyes droop shut. "It wasn't in his face just now—the hate. That was what I was waiting for, Sara. That was the start for Jimmie Joe."

The Classic Film Collection

The Searchers by Alan LeMay

Hailed as one of the greatest American films, *The Searchers,* directed by John Ford and starring John Wayne, has had a direct influence on the works of Martin Scorsese, Steven Spielberg, and many others. Its gorgeous cinematic scope and deeply nuanced characters have proven timeless. And now available for the first time in decades is the powerful novel that inspired this iconic movie.

Destry Rides Again by Max Brand

Made in 1939, the Golden Year of Hollywood, *Destry Rides Again* helped launch Jimmy Stewart's career and made Marlene Dietrich an American icon. Now available for the first time in decades is the novel that inspired this much-loved movie.

The Man from Laramie by T. T. Flynn

In its original publication, *The Man from Laramie* had more than half a million copies in print. Shortly thereafter, it became one of the most recognized of the Anthony Mann/Jimmy Stewart collaborations, known for darker films with morally complex characters. Now the novel upon which this classic movie was based is once again available—for the first time in more than fifty years.

The Unforgiven by Alan LeMay

In this epic American novel, which served as the basis for the classic film directed by John Huston and starring Burt Lancaster and Audrey Hepburn, a family is torn apart when an old enemy starts a vicious rumor that sets the range aflame. Don't miss the powerful novel that inspired the film the *Motion Picture Herald* calls "an absorbing and compelling drama of epic proportions."

To order a book or to request a catalog call:
1-800-481-9191
Books are also available at your local bookstore, or you can check out our Web site **www.dorchesterpub.com**.

Five-time Winner of the Spur Award

Will Henry

There is perhaps no outlaw of the Old West more notorious or legendary than Billy the Kid. And no author is better suited than Will Henry to tell the tale of the young gunman . . . and the mysterious stranger who changed his life.

Also included in this volume are two exciting novellas: "Santa Fe Passage" is the basis for the classic 1955 film of the same name. And "The Fourth Horseman" sets a rancher on the trail of a kidnapped young woman . . . while trying to survive a bloody range war.

A BULLET FOR BILLY THE KID

ISBN 13: 978-0-8439-6340-3

Bill Pronzini &
Marcia Muller

The dark clouds are gathering, and it's promising to be a doozy of a storm at the River Bend stage station . . . where the owners are anxiously awaiting the return of their missing daughter. Where a young cowboy hopes to find safety from the rancher whose wife he's run away with. Where a Pinkerton agent has tracked the quarry he's been chasing for years. Thunder won't be the only thing exploding along . . .

CRUCIFIXION RIVER

Bill Pronzini and Marcia Muller are a husband-wife writing team with numerous individual honors, including the Lifetime Achievement Award from the Private Eye Writers of America, the Grand Master Award from Mystery Writers of America, and the American Mystery Award. In addition to the Spur Award–winning title novella, this volume also contains stories featuring Bill Pronzini's famous "Nameless Detective" and Marcia Muller's highly popular Sharon McCone investigator.

ISBN 13: 978-0-8439-6341-0

A story so powerful that Clint Eastwood, who directed and starred in the 1976 film, has said it was his favorite movie to make.

The Outlaw Josey Wales

"A marathon chase that runs from Missouri to the Rio Grande, garnished with everything a Western outlaw could want. There are banks to rob, trusty sidekicks to ride with, blue-bellies to annihilate, and at the end of the trail a big surprise."
—*New York Times Book Review*

Josey Wales is out for blood. The Union Army slaughtered his family and lured his friends into a death trap under the guise of a white flag. The war may be over, but he refuses to surrender. No matter how far he has to ride, no matter how high the price on his head, no matter how much he hurts or hungers—he will get his vengeance.

Forrest Carter

ISBN 13: 978-0-8439-6346-5

COVERING THE OLD WEST
FROM COVER TO COVER.

Since 1953 we have been helping preserve the American West
with great original photos, true stories, new facts,
old facts and current events.

True West Magazine
We Make the Old West Addictive.

INTERACT WITH DORCHESTER ONLINE!

Want to learn more about your favorite
books and authors?
Want to talk with other readers that like
to read the same books as you?
Want to see up-to-the-minute Dorchester
news?

VISIT DORCHESTER AT:
DorchesterPub.com
Twitter.com/DorchesterPub
Facebook.com (Search Pages)

DISCUSS DORCHESTER'S
NOVELS AT:
Dorchester Forums at DorchesterPub.com
GoodReads.com
LibraryThing.com
Myspace.com/books
Shelfari.com
WeRead.com

☐ **YES!**

Sign me up for the Leisure Western Book Club and send my FREE BOOKS! If I choose to stay in the club, I will pay only $14.00* each month, a savings of $9.96!

NAME: _____

ADDRESS: _____

TELEPHONE: _____

EMAIL: _____

☐ I want to pay by credit card.

☐ **VISA**   ☐ **MasterCard.**   ☐ **DISCOVER**

ACCOUNT #: _____

EXPIRATION DATE: _____

SIGNATURE: _____

Mail this page along with $2.00 shipping and handling to:
Leisure Western Book Club
PO Box 6640
Wayne, PA 19087
Or fax (must include credit card information) to:
610-995-9274
You can also sign up online at **www.dorchesterpub.com**.
*Plus $2.00 for shipping. Offer open to residents of the U.S. and Canada only.
Canadian residents please call 1-800-481-9191 for pricing information.
If under 18, a parent or guardian must sign. Terms, prices and conditions subject to change. Subscription subject to acceptance. Dorchester Publishing reserves the right to reject any order or cancel any subscription.